THE
FALL
OF
FREEDOM

PAUL ORTON

PROLOGUE

I'm Zac.

The boy nobody trusts.

I risked my life sneaking into Arcadia to hack the network. The Resistance sent me to bring down the Collective and end the lockdown.

Things didn't go to plan.

They never do.

Now, I have too many secrets, things no one will believe. It's way too complicated, and I don't have time to explain.

What matters is this: We have to stop the Collective from distributing the Vicron-X vaccine to the rest of the population. That won't be what the Resistance wants to hear. But that vaccine has been poisoned, and once it's released, people will die.

I have no idea how to stop that from happening.

My name is Zac, and I'm a member of the Resistance.

My name is Zac, and I'm in way too deep.

ONE

I'm clinging to Kieran's waist as he powers the bike along the open road.

"Do you have to take the corners quite so fast?" I shout in his ear, my voice muffled by the helmet.

Kieran laughs. "We're making a getaway, remember?"

"Won't they send someone after us? What if there's a roadblock?"

"We're way up north. There are no roadblocks. Not on these roads. Too rural." He sweeps around another bend and I tighten my grip. "Are you trying to crush my ribs?"

"I'm trying to avoid becoming roadkill."

"Relax. You're always so uptight."

He's right. I am.

But that's hardly surprising. I've just escaped from the Arcadia development, the central headquarters of the Collective. Worse still, I know their deepest secrets and they're coming after me.

I'm a wanted boy.

I got over the fence with the help of a zeppelin, but I'm battered and bruised.

And tired.

I'm so tired.

I've been running on adrenaline for hours, and it's wearing off.

Outside the fence, they set the dogs on me. It's a good job Kieran rescued me on the dirt bike or I'd have been captured within minutes. But at least I wouldn't die in a terrible crash.

"Please ease off a bit. You're scaring me," I admit.

"It's not a road accident you need to be afraid of," he says. "It's Layla. What are you going to say to her?"

He's already told me she's mad. She's the leader of our Resistance cell and she thinks I failed my mission. Which I did. Sort of.

I ignore the question and swear under my

breath. "How far is it?"

"Not much further on the bike. We'll switch transport soon."

As far as I'm concerned, that can't come soon enough.

***

Kieran veers on to a dirt track through a forest, but doesn't slow down.

The path is bumpy, and I'm almost thrown from the seat. Before long, we're weaving between trees, snapping off twigs.

Finally, we come to a stop.

"We're here."

I climb off the bike and tug off my helmet. It takes my ears a while to adjust after the loud engine, but the woods aren't as peaceful as I expect.

"What's that?" I ask him.

"What's what?"

"That noise?"

"Chill, would you? It's just the river." He hauls the bike into some bushes. A tarpaulin is hidden beneath them. Kieran lays it over the bike, then heaps leaves on top. "Help me cover this."

"Sure." I kneel and get to work. "Do you do this a lot?"

"I've been keeping an eye on Arcadia for a while," he says. "I come most days."

"Where do you sleep?"

"In a Resistance base up here. That's where we're headed."

"I thought we'd go back to the pub." I'd been looking forward to seeing my old friends.

"That's miles away, idiot." He punches me on the arm. "We'll have to hope Cypher can find a way to get us back."

"Cypher?"

"He's the boss up here. And he's hardcore. Makes Layla look soft."

Kieran leads the way through the trees, sweat glistening on his black forehead. He's much bigger than me and he looks like a trained mercenary, not a boy of fourteen. That's what the lockdown has done to him.

I still look like a kid, but I'm no less of a man. We've lost our adolescent years. We're not boys, we're soldiers.

The river is getting louder. As we push

through the undergrowth, we emerge next to it. A muddy bank leads down to the fast-flowing water.

"How do we cross?" I ask.

Kieran smiles. "We go down the river, not over it." He walks over to another bush and reaches underneath. He hauls something out: a kayak.

I glance at the narrow craft and then at the rough water. "You're not serious."

"Afraid so." He throws me a helmet. "Just to warn you, it's a bit of a wild ride."

"Worse than the bike?"

He grins as if I've said something funny. It's hardly reassuring.

"Have you been in one of these before?" he asks.

"A couple of times," I admit. "They had them in Arcadia."

"So, you know how to use the paddle?"

"I guess. But the lake there was calm. Nothing like this."

"Rough water's a lot more fun," he says, balancing the kayak on the bank. "Avoid the rocks and try not to fall in."

I can't tell if he's joking.

It turns out he's not.

TWO

The kayak plunges down, splashing me with water.

We've only been in the river for two minutes, and I'm already soaked through. The skintight active wear might have got ripped during my escape, but it keeps me warm. It's either that, or the amount of paddling I'm doing, trying to keep us moving in the right direction and away from the rocks.

"I told you this was fun," shouts Kieran, over the noise of the river.

"I'm done with fun," I yell back. "I just want sleep."

"That's what I missed, Zac. Your adventurous spirit."

I suppress a smile.

"We're drifting to the left," I point out. "You need to paddle harder."

"Hey, don't sweat. Go with the flow. Until we get to the rapids, anyway."

"The rapids?" I'm hoping that's another of his jokes.

"Rapids is an exaggeration, to be fair. But there are some nasty rocks and the water gets a bit churned up."

I look around me at the fast-flowing eddies and the white froth. "You're telling me this is the calm stretch?"

"You'll see."

I don't want to see. I've experienced enough danger today to last a lifetime, but as we navigate our way around a bend, sharp rocks jut out of the water ahead.

"We need to focus," says Kieran. "This can get dicey."

"No kidding."

"Go hard left," he shouts, plunging his paddle deep.

I copy him, forcing the kayak towards a narrow gap in the rocks.

"That's good, Zac," shouts Kieran, "now a

touch to the right."

"Okay." I sweep my paddle down on the other side of the boat, but it doesn't have the desired effect. The back of the kayak is swinging around and if we don't do something fast, we're going to be the wrong way around when we hit the rapids.

"No!" shouts Kieran. He sounds worried now. "We're losing control!"

"I'm on it." I swing my paddle around and plunge it deep into the churning water.

Disaster! It gets caught between two rocks. I try to pull it free, but the kayak is moving so fast that I'm worried I'll get dragged from the boat. My body is being stretched over the white froth, and I hook my feet around the seat in the kayak to stop it pulling away.

"What the hell are you doing?" Kieran shouts as he twists around.

I don't have time to answer. I've lost my balance. Worse still, I somehow capsize the kayak as I fall out, pulling him into the water behind me.

Now we're both carried along by the river, dragged towards the rocks. We try to swim, but there's not much point. The water throws us around like rag dolls, first this way, then the other.

Before long, I can't see Kieran.

I can't see anything. My face is underwater and everything is brown. A stream of white bubbles rises in front of me. That's the air from my lungs as I breathe out.

Unless I can get to the surface, I'm going to die.

I bang my head on a rock, then use my legs to push away. I need air.

Somehow, I break the surface.

I take a frantic gasp before being sucked back down. My body is spinning; I don't even know which way is up.

I'm exhausted.

I can't go on.

I close my eyes and let the river take me.

Everything goes black.

***

Something weird is happening.

Someone is kissing me.

That's what it feels like, anyway.

I open my eyes to find Kieran's face up close. As soon as he sees I'm awake, he pulls away. I try to say something, but there's water in my mouth and I roll over and spew it out. I rest on my elbow, coughing and retching until my airways are clear.

Kieran is wiping his mouth. "I can't believe you made me do that."

"Did you... did you just save my life?"

"Someone has to, but if you pull another stunt like that, I'll let you drown. I'm not kissing your ugly mug again." He gives me a dark look. "No one hears about this. Ever."

"Fine by me." I breathe deep. Oxygen has never tasted so good.

"You lost the kayak," says Kieran. He's not teasing me; he's properly annoyed. "It floated down the river."

"I didn't mean to. My paddle got stuck."

"You could have let it go. We had another. You know what we don't have?"

"Another kayak."

"That's right, Zac. Thanks to you, we just lost our only boat. So now, we're cold, wet and have miles to walk. I hope you're happy."

"It wasn't deliberate." I pull off my trainers and empty out the water. Kieran gives me a weird look as I do it. "What?"

"Are those actual tights?" he says. He's staring at my feet. "Like girls wear?"

"They're more like sportswear. Everyone wears them in Arcadia."

"If you say so." That gets him thinking. "What was it like?"

I think back to my time inside the compound. "It's as beautiful as it looked in the pictures. People live in log cabins and tree-houses in the woods. There's some other buildings too where we had school and stuff."

He smirks at that. "You had to go to school?"

I pull the trainers back on. "Yeah, it was hard work. You barely get any free time there. Everyone stays busy. They think they're saving the world."

"By keeping the vaccine to themselves? How do they figure that? My dad and brother died from the virus because they were so selfish."

"They think Vicron-X isn't the biggest problem." I stand up and face him. "The bigger problem is climate change, and if they release the vaccine, we'll lose control of global warming."

"What are you talking about?"

"Before the lockdown, we were killing the planet. Now, things are back under control. But the moment a vaccine is released, everyone will start to poison the atmosphere again. And then we'll all die. That's what they reckon, anyway."

He gives me a suspicious look. "You don't believe them, do you?"

"I don't know," I admit. "They made a good point. It seemed pretty believable while I was there."

He shakes his head like I'm nuts. "Sounds like you were in that place too long."

"Maybe."

"Let's start the long hike to base. If we stick to the bank, we shouldn't get lost."

"Sure, I guess, but I need a little longer to recover. My lungs are on fire."

He only gives me another ten minutes, before he drags me to my feet, urging me on. He leads the way, staying close to the river.

As I squelch along behind him, every part of my body hurts. I'm puffing and panting like an old man. "Will it take long to get there?"

"It would have been a lot quicker in a kayak." He's still upset about that.

"How long?" I ask again.

"Why? You got somewhere you need to be?"

"Not exactly. But the people in Arcadia are about to release the vaccine."

Kieran turns to me, his eyes shining. "So? That's awesome news."

I shake my head. "Trust me, it's not. It's a fake. It'll kill everyone. The entire population."

"I thought you said these people were trying to save the world."

I swallow hard. "It's complicated."

"In that case, we'd better hurry." Kieran sets off at a faster pace. "But bro, you've got some serious explaining to do."

I know he's right.

But I doubt anyone will want to hear what I have to say.

THREE

It's getting dark as we trudge up a steep hill.

"Surely, it can't be much further?" I whine. My legs ache and I don't think I can walk another mile.

"We're nearly there."

We haven't seen any sign of civilisation. But as we emerge from the trees, I see a building straight ahead. It's like a fairytale castle built out of dark stone. Instinctively, I crouch down behind a bush. "How do we get past that place without being seen?"

Kieran tugs on my arm. "We don't. That's the Resistance base."

"The castle?"

"It's called Rushfell Hall."

"How do they stay hidden in *that*?"

Kieran grins at me. "They don't have to. As far as the world is concerned, the Rushfell family are living there with their house and grounds staff. Bit different from living in an abandoned pub, eh?"

"That place and the pub have one thing in common," I point out.

"Yeah? What's that?"

"They both look like they belong in a horror movie."

That makes Kieran laugh. He slaps me on the back. "It's much more comfortable inside. But there's something you should know before we go in."

"What?"

"It's Cypher. He's a bit weird."

"In what way?"

"You'll see. Just try not to wind him up."

Kieran strides towards the huge front door. He climbs several stone steps, then presses a button for an intercom. I hang back a little, used to hiding in the shadows.

"What is your purpose here?" asks a metallic voice.

"It's Kieran. Long live the Resistance!"

The door opens. A middle-aged man stands there in full army gear.

"Hey, Nash," says Kieran. "I'm back."

Nash smiles at him, then catches sight of me. "Who's your friend?"

"Zac. He escaped Arcadia."

Realisation dawns on the man's face. "I've heard a lot about you, Zac. It's good to meet you in person. Come up here. I'd better take you to Cypher."

Encouraged by the warm welcome, I climb the steps. We're led through a grand hallway full of antique furniture and old paintings. Everywhere smells of brass and polished wood. The man knocks on a door at the far end, then opens it without waiting for a response. We follow him into a large dining room with a table that stretches from one end to another. You could seat at least thirty people around it.

There's no one in here except a man who stands at the far end of the room, looking out of a large bay window. He's wearing a long black overcoat that hangs down to shiny black boots.

"Kieran's back, sir. And he's brought Zac," announces Nash.

"Thank you, Nash. You may leave." Cypher doesn't even turn around. As soon as the door closes, he speaks again. "You're late."

Kieran gulps. "Sorry, sir."

"Sorry isn't a reason." Now the man spins around. He stalks towards us at an alarming speed. His face is messed up; one side covered in shiny metal, making him appear more robot than human. "According to my calculations, you should have been here four and a half hours ago."

"We ran into some difficulties with the kayak." Kieran glances over at me. "I'm afraid we lost it. We had to walk most of the way."

Cypher stares at Kieran for a while, his expression cold. "I should have you punished."

"It was my fault," I blurt out. "Don't blame him."

"Is that so?" Cypher steps towards me. Where his right eye should be, there's some kind of camera lens with a glowing red light, but his human eye is pale blue like ice. "Zachary David McAllister."

I don't know whether to be impressed or freaked out that he's somehow found out my middle name. "That's me."

"The boy everyone has been hoping would hack the Collective network."

I shuffle my feet. "Yeah."

"But you didn't."

"It wasn't as easy as we expected. The Arcadia network is off-grid. Most of it, anyway. Please, I need to speak to Layla."

"I am in charge here."

"It's urgent. The Collective are going to release the vaccine. But it's not really the vaccine. It'll kill everyone. Everyone outside Arcadia, anyway."

Cypher stares at me like I'm mad. "That's highly improbable."

"Improbable or not, it's the truth!"

"So you say."

"You don't have to believe me. I just need to speak to her."

"That would be an error." Cypher tilts his head to one side. "You seem hysterical. You've spent a long time in enemy territory. We don't know that they haven't turned you, or brainwashed you. This could be a trap."

"They haven't. I'm telling the truth. You need to take me to Layla."

Without warning, Cypher slaps me hard

around the face, knocking me to the floor. "Learn some respect, boy. I decide what action we take."

I brush the back of my mouth with my arm, smearing it with blood.

Kieran steps forward. "Sir, Zac is the most honest boy I know. He wouldn't lie about this."

"There's only one way to find out. Fetch Dr Viega."

"But sir..."

Cypher cuts him off with the wave of a hand. "One more word and I'll have you thrown in solitary. Do as I say."

Kieran salutes and heads out the door.

I might have imagined it, but I think I saw fear in his eyes.

FOUR

Dr Viega looks more like a business executive than a medic. He wears a smart grey suit and carries a brown briefcase, which he slams down on the table.

He peers at me through thick glasses. At least, I think that's what he's doing; he's cross-eyed, so it's hard to tell exactly where his gaze lands.

"Sit down." The doctor gestures to a chair. Over his shoulder, Kieran hovers near the door. He gives me a small nod, encouraging me to follow the man's instructions.

I drop into the seat, wondering what's about to happen.

Dr Viega opens his briefcase. He reaches inside and pulls out some kind of metallic headband. He hands it to me, wires trailing from the device back to the case. "Put this on."

I examine it. It looks like something from an old science-fiction movie. "What is it?"

"It checks you're telling the truth," cuts in Cypher. He's standing right behind me, breathing down my neck. "There's nothing to be afraid of. Unless you're a liar."

I slip the band over my hair. It's too big and falls down to rest on my ears. The doctor takes hold of it and makes some adjustments, twisting and pulling until it feels too tight, the metal cold against my forehead.

He looks up at Cypher. "I have to check the settings before we begin the interrogation."

Interrogation?

I don't like the sound of that. "Hey, we're on the same side."

"We'll see," mutters Cypher. He strides around the long table so he can see the readings on the screen inside the briefcase.

"State your full name," says Dr Viega.

"Zachary David McAllister." I say it slowly and carefully, worried that I might even get this wrong.

"Good. Now I want you to tell us a lie. What

colour is this pen?" The doctor holds up a blue pen in his hand.

"Red," I say.

Dr Viega nods, satisfied. He points something out to Cypher. "That's a clear negative. He should be easy to read."

I gulp. I'm not sure that's a good thing. But if it means they'll believe me when I tell them about the poisoned vaccine, then it'll be worth it.

Cypher straightens up and looks me in the eye. "I'm going to ask you some questions now, and I want nothing but the truth. Do you understand?"

"Yes, sir."

"Who are you working for?"

"Layla. And the Resistance."

Cypher carries on: "You went into Arcadia to get access to the Collective's network, right?"

"That's right."

"But you failed."

I wince. "It wasn't possible. They have more than one network. The main one isn't even connected to the internet. And the other is kept secure."

"But you did try?" pushes Cypher. "You *wanted* to break in?"

"Sure. Of course."

At that, Dr Viega points something out. Even Kieran raises his eyebrows.

"Did you have some doubts about the mission, Zac?" asks Cypher.

"No."

Cypher glances inside the briefcase. "You're lying."

"Ok, I had *some* doubts," I admit.

"Why?"

"The Collective are trying to save the world."

"How?" demands Cypher.

"They're keeping everyone in lockdown to prevent climate change."

"That's what they told you?"

"Yes, sir."

"And you believed them?" The artificial eye rotates a little as he stares at me.

"They had a point," I allow. "What they were saying made sense."

"DID YOU BELIEVE THEM?" Cypher shouts across the table.

I look away. "I believed Aaron Greaves, the founder. He seemed like a good guy."

"Did Aaron Greaves know who you were?"

"Just before I escaped, he admitted that he'd known all along."

"So, he knew you were part of the Resistance?"

I nod.

"You have to say it," points out Dr Viega.

"Yes. He knew who I was. The whole thing was a set-up."

Cypher pulls out a chair and sits down, facing me across the table. "Surely you realise they played you, Zac? They knew who you were from the start."

I stay silent. I'm too embarrassed to admit he might be right.

He presses on. "Have they developed a vaccine to Vicron-X?"

"Yes, everyone in Arcadia is immune."

"But they've kept it to themselves for years."

"Yes," I mumble.

"And now they're planning to release it?" asks Cypher.

"Not the real one. A poisoned one. They want to kill everyone on the outside."

"Why would they do that? I thought you said they were good people?"

"Some of them are. Most of them. But there's

been a change of leadership. The new guy, Eugene, believes that the bigger issue is climate change and the only way we can save the planet is by wiping out most of the population."

"And Aaron Greaves is okay with that?"

"No. That's why they arrested him. Just before I escaped."

"How convenient." Cypher pulls a face and rubs his chin. "You can see how this looks, Zac. By their own admission, they knew who you were. They've somehow convinced you that the vaccine is poisoned and then let you escape so you could tell us about it."

"It's not like that," I insist. "It wasn't easy to get out."

"That's what they'd want you to think. But you're only a kid and you escaped. And they've got inside your head, and persuaded you to tell us we need to destroy the vaccine because it's so dangerous."

"But why would they want me to tell you that?" I ask, exasperated. "If it isn't true?"

"Several reasons," explains Cypher. "Maybe, despite their considerable influence, the Collective couldn't stop the vaccine being produced, so they want us to destroy it. Or maybe they want the wider population to turn against the Resistance."

"That vaccine is deadly," I insist. "You have to stop it."

"The Collective certainly convinced you of their lies."

"They're not lies! Your machine should tell you that!"

Cypher gestures at the briefcase. "All this tells me is that you believe what you're saying. It doesn't mean it's true."

I lean back. "You're not going to destroy it?"

"The world needs that vaccine. We've been waiting for years. The last thing we want to do is blow it up."

"Please let me speak with Layla," I moan. I need to explain this to someone who will listen. Cypher just thinks I'm some gullible kid.

"You'll just confuse her." Cypher turns to face Kieran. "You agree, don't you? You've heard everything just now. The Collective have brainwashed your friend."

I look at Kieran, hoping he'll put up a fight.

"Zac's being an idiot," he says, with a shrug.

"It's not his fault. He's been in Arcadia for way too long. Who knows what they did to him in there? Give him a few weeks and he'll see sense."

That hurts. It really hurts.

Even Kieran doesn't believe me.

Cypher nods, satisfied. He turns back to me. "I'm going to keep you locked up for now until the vaccine has been distributed. I can't allow your dangerous delusions to affect our operations. And if I let you wander free, I know you'll try to contact Layla. Or even escape so you can destroy the vaccine."

"I won't!" I shout.

That must give a massive negative reading because Cypher smiles. Well, the human side of his face does. "There's no point lying, Zac. If I believed what you believe, I'd do the same. We're going to keep you under lock and key for your own safety."

Tears run down my cheeks. "If you do this, everyone will die."

"Do you know how crazy you sound?" says Kieran, shaking his head with disappointment.

Cypher leans back. "We'll keep you in the east tower. Once the vaccine is out, I'll return you to

Layla and your friends down south."

"You'll be dead by then," I point out. "The vaccine will have killed you all."

Cypher waves the danger away with his hand. "We'll see."

FIVE

Nash takes me up a spiral staircase. We stop near the top of the tower and he pushes open a heavy wooden door.

I'm expecting the place to look like a dungeon, but I'm pleasantly surprised. There's a four-poster bed in here and a private bathroom. I should be comfortable at least. There's even a large window with an amazing view across the valley.

"I know what you're thinking," says Nash. "You're wondering if you can escape, but we're four floors up. Take a look."

I shuffle over to the window. It's a straight drop to the ground.

"Someone will stand guard outside your door."

"I'm not the enemy," I point out. "Haven't you got better things to do?"

"Listen, lad, you've got a rough deal. I get it. But I'm just following orders and in a few weeks this will all be sorted out."

"If by *sorted out*, you mean everyone will be dead."

Nash shakes his head as if I'm beyond reason. "They really convinced you, didn't they?"

"Maybe I'm not so gullible. Maybe it's true."

"No point arguing with me, lad," laughs Nash. "You just try to make yourself comfortable."

With that, he leaves, pulling the door closed behind him. I hear a key turn in the lock.

Everything is silent, except for the ticking of a clock on the bedside table. That makes it worse. I'll be reminded every second that I'm running out of time. I wander around the room, opening cupboards and checking drawers. They're all empty; they haven't left anything I can use to escape.

But I have to get out.

I'm the only person outside Arcadia who knows what's about to happen, who knows the vaccine is lethal. I have to destroy it, whatever it takes.

Still, there's nothing I can do right now except take a shower. My escape from Arcadia and swimming in the river have left me sweaty and grimy. It feels good to let the hot water wash it all away. I wish I could wash away my tiredness as well.

Sadly, I don't have any clean clothes so I have to pull on my Arcadia gear. I've barely got dressed before there's a knock at the door.

"What is it?" I ask.

Kieran walks in holding a tray with pastries and jam. "I brought you some food."

My mouth waters but I turn away. "I thought we were friends. You called me a liar in there."

"That's not true." Kieran puts down the tray and glances behind him, checking the door. "I just think Cypher's right. What you're saying doesn't make sense."

"So, I'm an idiot?"

"No, Zac. You've just been duped. The Collective are clever, we know that."

Out of the corner of my eye, I see him lifting his T-shirt. A climbing rope is coiled around his waist and he unravels it as fast as he can.

"What..." I begin, but he cuts me off, putting his finger to his lips.

"What I'm saying is that you need some time to sleep it off, to come to your senses." He's speaking loudly, making sure that whoever's guarding the room can hear. "Cypher is a genius. You have to trust him." He uncoils the last of the rope and stuffs it under the pillow.

"I can't believe you're siding with him!" I shout, but I wink at him as I do it. Kieran isn't on their side at all. He's helping me escape.

"He's the leader. Even Layla obeys his orders," explains Kieran.

"Well, she can get lost. And so can you. I hate you." I yell the last bit, making it sound believable.

"If you're sure." Kieran backs towards the door. "Try to eat something, Zac. It'll make you feel better. And try some of the jam. It's amazing." He gives me a meaningful look, but he's interrupted as a guard opens the door to check on us.

"That's enough talk, lads," says the soldier.

Kieran shrugs and leaves without another word. "I tried reasoning with him," he mutters to the guard, "but he won't listen."

The door slams, leaving me alone.

Now, I have food.

And I have a rope.

Best of all, I still have a friend I can trust.

***

Under the jam is a note: "I'll meet you outside at 2am. Use the rope to get down."

That makes it sound easy.

Sure, Kieran, I don't mind climbing out of a four-storey window.

Still, I don't have a better plan so I have to push it to the back of my mind. When the time comes, I'll face my fear. Until then, I don't want to think about it.

I try to grab some sleep, but I keep tossing and turning, checking the clock every few minutes. I can't find any way to set an alarm and I'm worried I'll sleep past two.

Also, there's a lot on my mind.

After the interrogation, I'm starting to wonder if I really am being gullible, believing what I've been told about the vaccine.

When I heard about the poison, it all seemed so real. But if no one else believes it, what am I meant to think? Are they all stupid, or am I?

At quarter to two, I get ready. I tie the rope to the four-poster bed, knotting it several times. I figure that's got to be heavy enough to take my weight. Once I've made it safe, I open the window and lean out.

It's pitch black out there, the moon obscured by cloud. I turn off the light in my room, allowing my eyes to adjust to the darkness. There's no sign of Kieran.

Regardless, I can't wait any longer. It's now or never. The longer I look at the drop, the less confidence I have.

I'm sure there's some brilliant method you can use to climb down a rope. The problem is, I don't know it. I just grip as tightly as I can, and ease my body out. Little by little, I shimmy down. By the time I'm halfway, my hands are burning. They're getting cut to pieces, but I can't let go, so I ignore the pain and press on. I feel like I'm in the gym lesson from hell. If I fall, I die. Knowing that sure helps me to focus.

Get it done, Zac.

I keep going. This must be the slowest escape attempt in history.

After a while, I check how far I am from the ground. It's not far. I can drop the last few metres. Taking a deep breath, I let go of the rope and fall into the long grass, bending my knees and rolling forwards as soon as I make impact.

"You could be in the Olympics." Kieran is standing over me, grinning.

I groan and sit up. "Thanks for the rope," I whisper. "But next time, could you find one that doesn't rip my hands to shreds?" I lift my palms to show him, even though he can't see anything in the darkness.

"Noted. If I have to rescue you again, I'll ask our enemies for a nice soft rope. Or maybe a ladder. That's not likely to make them suspicious."

I punch him on the arm. "What do we do now?"

"We get the hell out of here, before they realise we've gone. If they catch us, they'll break both our legs."

Having met Cypher, I'm not even sure if he's exaggerating.

He leads the way down the hill, moving as quickly as he dares. I follow close behind. We both feel a lot better once we reach the trees.

"There's a village near here," he says. "The best plan is to break into someone's house and contact Layla."

"So, you believe me?" I ask.

He hesitates. "I don't know what to believe, if I'm honest. But you're a mate and I think Layla needs to hear what you've got to say. She knows you're not daft."

"Thanks for rescuing me."

"Yeah, well someone's got to. For a good kid, you sure get into a lot of trouble."

"I blame the people I hang out with."

That makes him laugh.

We wander for a while, making slow progress through the undergrowth.

"Kieran?" I ask. "Do you think Layla will believe me? Will she help us stop the vaccine?"

"I don't know," he admits. "If you're right about this, I hope so, or we're screwed."

"Us and everyone else," I mutter.

I don't mention it, but that includes my mum and my brother, who were locked up for helping the Resistance. If I fail, they'll die.

That thought keeps me grounded.

And even more determined to succeed.

SIX

Kieran moves fast, and I struggle to keep up.

"We need to be careful when we reach the village," he says. "If they find out we've escaped, it'll be the first place they look."

"Wait up." I pause for a moment to catch my breath. "They won't realise I'm missing until the morning."

"We can't hang around, just in case. We have to get a message to Layla now."

"Have you got a plan?"

"We're going to break into a house. I know how much you enjoy that." He gives me a shove. "Just try not to knock over any vases."

"I'll do my best."

When Kieran and I first met, I'd broken into his house and done exactly that. I had no idea we'd become such close friends. That all happened so long ago that it doesn't seem real.

The trees thin out and we approach the edge of the village.

Before we get too close, Kieran pulls me back. "We're looking for a house with a kid or a teenager," he mutters.

"Why?" I ask. "What difference does it make?"

"We need to find someone who we can overpower if they wake up, and who has access to a decent computer. Unless you think you can take on someone twice your size?"

I'm a skinny kid, and while he's a lot more solid than me, even he might lose a fight against an adult.

But I don't want to do this at all; the thought of sneaking in to someone's house and holding them hostage makes me feel like one of the bad guys.

We creep through the village. The houses are all cloaked in darkness; it's too late for anyone to be awake.

Kieran grabs my arm and points. I can't see why he's interested; the house he's pointing at looks pretty standard.

Then I see it: a rusty basketball hoop attached to the wall.

We move closer. The fence around the back garden isn't all that high and we can climb over. The patio curtains haven't been drawn and we peer in, trying to make out shapes in the darkness.

"Can you see anything?" I whisper.

"Not much. But I'd recognise that purple light anywhere. Just below the TV."

I check it out. Kieran's right. Whoever lives here has got a decent games console. "I wonder if they've got *Fields of War*."

"You sucked at that game." Kieran grins, his teeth gleaming in the darkness. "I wiped the floor with you every time we played."

"I still miss it." I long to go back to the days when my biggest worry was whether I was going to lose an online tournament. "How do we get in?"

"No idea," admits Kieran. "I thought that was your area of expertise."

I step back and check out the windows. It doesn't look promising. But then I see above the single-storey garage. "They've left a window open. Probably the bathroom."

There's a bench we can lift and, once it's next to the wall, Kieran boosts me up on to the garage roof. I pull him up behind me. We're staying quiet, but even the slightest noise makes me cringe. I keep my eye on the windows to see if anyone has heard us.

Nothing.

We make our way over to the open window.

"It's tiny," hisses Kieran. "You sure you'll fit through that?"

"I'm a pro, remember? Give me a leg up. Once I'm in, I'll try to open the door for you."

He lifts me so I can open the window a little wider, then pull my body through. It's a tight squeeze, but it's much easier doing this in the active wear from Arcadia than it would be in normal clothes. Once inside, I balance on the side of the bath and lower myself to the floor.

I listen, checking I haven't woken anyone. There's a strange noise, like a grunting or growling coming from one of the bedrooms. I panic, wondering if they have a dog, but realise it's just the sound of someone snoring.

So far, so good.

I creep down the stairs, taking it slow in case they creak. I don't weigh much and I keep my feet close to the edges where they're least likely to make any noise. When I reach the back door, I'm relieved to see the key. Seconds later, Kieran is standing next to me in the kitchen.

Now comes the hard part. We have to somehow get access to the internet without waking anyone. We hunt around the lounge, but there's no sign of a computer.

"Must be in one of the bedrooms," mutters Kieran.

We climb the stairs. I can hear Kieran's heavy breathing over my shoulder. One door has a "KEEP OUT" sign and is ajar.

I slip inside. It's even darker in here, but it smells of sweat. Posters with tatty corners line the walls. Clothes are strewn across the floor. Someone is asleep in the bed. I move closer to look. It's just a young lad, can't be any older than twelve. His face looks angelic. I can't help wishing I had a life like his, without a care in the world.

Then I think back: living in lockdown wasn't fun. You weren't allowed out, and you still had to log on to school every day. Supplies were limited: you couldn't even get the food you wanted. Just because he looks safe and happy doesn't mean he has a good life. He's imprisoned here, in his own house.

"We're in luck." Kieran breathes the words in my ear, holding up a laptop.

"Switch it on," I hiss back. "See if it needs a password."

He looks at me, confused. "Can't you hack it?"

"It'll take too long."

He sits down on a chair and flips it open, hitting the power button. There's a soft ping as the laptop boots up but the boy doesn't stir. Kieran twists it around so I can see the login screen. We're going to need a password after all.

"Any ideas how we get him to tell us what it is?" I whisper to Kieran.

"Just one." Kieran pulls out a knife.

He leans over the bed and clamps his hand over the boy's mouth.

The lad jerks awake; his eyes go wide as sees Kieran. He tries to wriggle free, but Kieran is kneeling on his body.

Kieran holds the knife in front of the boy's

face. "Stay quiet, or I'll slit your throat. If you wake your parents, I'll kill them as well."

Tears well up in the boy's eyes.

I feel sorry for the kid. He doesn't deserve this, but we need that password. I do my best to reassure him. "You don't need to be afraid. We won't hurt you. Not unless you try to make any noise. Got it?"

The boy gives a small nod.

"All we need is the password to your laptop. We want to use it for a while. Then, we'll leave you in peace. I promise."

Kieran can see that I'm getting through to the boy. He speaks much softer this time. "I'm going to take my hand away now, but if you shout or make any noise, I'll kill you. I don't want to, but I will. Do you understand?"

The boy nods again.

Kieran removes his hand from the boy's mouth, ready to clamp it back in place if the kid makes any attempt to scream.

"Tell us the password," I say, gently.

"I-I-It's Liverpool dash t-t-twenty twenty," whimpers the boy.

"In numbers? Two zero, two zero?" I clarify.

The boy nods.

"See, that wasn't too hard," says Kieran, ruffling the kid's hair.

But Kieran has spoken too soon.

Because when I type in the password, it doesn't work.

SEVEN

"It won't accept it," I hiss.

"What are you playing at?" demands Kieran, holding the knife up to the kid's face. "You think this is a game? Tell me the wrong password again, and I'll chop off your ear."

He's bluffing. At least, I hope he is.

The boy lets out a muffled sob. "I'm telling the truth. Liverpool dash twenty twenty."

"Is it all lower-case?" I ask.

The boy nods.

"It's still not working," I say.

Kieran leans closer to the lad, a menacing look on his face. I have no idea what he's about to do.

"Wait," I say. "What kind of dash? Like a hyphen? Show me." I turn the laptop towards him. He points at the underscore.

This time, it works.

"It's ok," I tell Kieran. "We're in."

"Get up. You're coming with us." Kieran tugs the kid out of bed.

The boy's legs are shaking and there's a wet patch on his pyjamas. He's going to need serious therapy when we've gone.

We head downstairs, Kieran holding the knife against our captive's throat. I'm not sure he needs to; it feels like overkill. But it seems to work, so I don't object.

"You do whatever you need to do," Kieran says to me. "I'm taking this guy to the shed. I don't want him waking the rest of the house the minute we leave."

"Okay." I settle down in the lounge and get to work. The laptop is already connected to the net, so it only takes seconds for me to access the domain I use to contact the Resistance.

After a few seconds, Howard's face appears on the screen. He's one of the Resistance hackers, and he taught me most of what I know. He squints at me through his thick spectacles. "Is that you, Zac?"

"For sure. I need to speak with Layla. It's

urgent."

"She's on a mission."

I curse, frustrated. "Can you take a message for me? Tell her that the Collective are planning to poison everyone with a fake vaccine. We need to stop them."

Howard frowns. "You're sure about this?"

"A hundred per cent. But I'm stuck up north with Kieran, and Cypher doesn't believe me. He tried to lock me up."

"It seems highly unlikely."

I'm sick of people saying that. I hiss at him, worried that someone in the house might hear if I speak too loudly. "Listen, Howard, I'm the only one who's been inside Arcadia, right? I know what I'm talking about. This is urgent. If we don't destroy that vaccine, everyone will die."

"Okay," allows Howard, still not sounding convinced. He taps away on his keyboard. "If what you're saying is true, then we don't have much time. They've been stocking up on the vaccine. The first batch is about to be shipped to the continent. Crates are being taken to the docks as we speak. Once that shipment leaves, you'll never get it back."

"Which docks?" I demand.

"Huckstanton."

I open a new tab and pull it up on a map. "We'll try to get there," I say, "but we're going to need help."

"Even when she returns, I don't think Layla will assist. Cypher won't let her."

"So, what the hell are we meant to do?"

Howard squints at another screen. The man is as eccentric as they come, but he's one of the best hackers on the planet. "I've just zeroed in on your current location. If I wanted to get to the docks from there, I'd be going by train."

I wonder if he's been holed up in his room for too long. "You're a funny man, Howard. But the country is still in lockdown. There are no trains, remember?"

He shakes his head. "No passenger trains, true. But supplies are still being shipped around the country by rail. A freight train is scheduled to pass through the village of Deerford, not far from your location, at 10.26am tomorrow. If you could get on it, it's heading straight to the docks."

"I don't suppose you could ship me some explosives to the same location?"

Howard rubs his face. "You're on your own with this, I'm afraid. Even I can't go against Cypher's orders."

"I thought you guys were rebels," I point out.

"We're meant to be protecting the vaccine, not destroying it," he counters.

"It's not the vaccine. It's poison."

Howard looks at me, sadly. "We only have your word for that."

"But you trust me, right?"

Howard sighs. "I don't trust anyone."

***

I end the call and head downstairs. As I pass through the kitchen, I hunt around for some food. There's a pack of chocolate biscuits in a tin and I take them outside. Kieran is standing by the shed door.

"What did you do with the kid?" I ask, tearing open the pack.

Kieran grabs the first biscuit before he answers. "Take a look."

I peer inside and see the boy lying on the floor, bound and gagged with industrial tape. He's not going anywhere.

"Are we leaving him out here?"

"It's only a few hours until daylight, and it's not that cold. His parents will find him in the morning. How did you get on? Is Layla sending the cavalry?"

"Afraid not." As we munch our biscuits, I tell him about the conversation with Howard. "Looks like we're on our own."

"So, what do we do?" asks Kieran.

"We go to the docks ourselves. See if we can stop that shipment before it leaves."

"But how will stopping one shipment help?"

"According to Howard, until it arrives in other countries, the rest of the product is being kept at the laboratory where it's manufactured. They're trying to synchronise the rollout. So, if we can hit both those targets, we can destroy it all. The first batch anyway. And it'll take them weeks to make more, so it'll buy us enough time to warn everyone."

"That's okay then," says Kieran, drily. "That sounds easy now you've put it like that. Did Howard say how we can destroy it?"

"No, but he did tell us we should catch a train.

It'll be passing near here tomorrow morning."

"How near?"

"Twenty-seven miles," I admit. "We better get going or we'll have no chance. It's a long way to run."

Kieran looks at me, a smile forming on his lips. Then, he disappears inside the shed. When he comes out, he's wheeling a bike. "There are two of these in there," he says. "Do you think they'll help?"

I grin. "Just a bit."

EIGHT

We zoom down the open road, leaving the village far behind. Moving at this speed, we should reach our destination with hours to spare. I might even get some sleep before we try to board the train.

Not that I have any idea how we'll do that.

One problem at a time, Zac.

Right now, we need to get to Deerford before the train. Once we're there, I'll come up with a plan.

Kieran races ahead like he's in the Tour de France. I'm glad I made him wear a helmet. But as I try to keep up, I see him skid to a halt.

I pull up behind. "What is it?"

"Something's coming this way." He points down the road and now that I'm still I can hear a vehicle in the distance. "I can't see any headlights, so it's not the Quarantine Agency."

"Who, then?" I ask, confused.

"It could be the Resistance. Cypher might have discovered we've gone."

The stretch of road we're on isn't exactly full of potential hiding places. On one side of us is a small grassy bank leading to a thick hedge. On the other is a high stone wall.

"I don't think we can squeeze under that," I say. "And the wall is much too high. We don't have time. And there's nowhere to hide the bikes."

Kieran puts his foot on the pedal. "In that case, let's move."

"You're not planning to outrun them?"

"A short way back, we passed the entrance to a field. We could hide in there." He kicks off, pedalling furiously. I follow him, cursing.

This isn't good.

I keep glancing behind me, sure that any second now I'll see a car over my shoulder. Whenever I twist my head, I can hear the engine getting closer.

Then, I glimpse it.

At least, I think I do. There's a dark shape in

the distance.

"They're nearly on us," I puff.

"Follow me." Kieran veers off the road without warning, through an open gate into a field.

I do as he says, gripping the handlebars as the bike judders over the rough terrain. We're going way too fast and I know this won't end well.

Sure enough, seconds later I hit a large bump that sends me flying. The bike crashes down and I end up sprawled face-down in the mud.

Kieran is only a few feet away, his bike lying on the floor next to him, the wheels still spinning.

"Stay down and stay quiet," he says.

The vehicle is getting closer. The engine is so loud, I wonder if it's going to drive into the field and run us over. But then it passes, continuing along the narrow lane.

I breathe a sigh of relief. "That was close."

"Too close," replies Kieran. "If he'd had his lights on, he'd have seen us. Are you okay?"

"I think so." I climb to my feet. "But every part of me hurts."

"We'd best keep moving."

"You sure it's safe?" I ask.

Kieran doesn't lie. "It's never safe," he replies.

***

The sky is grey by the time we reach Deerford.

It's a quiet village. The train line passes straight through the middle. There's even a deserted station.

Kieran stands on the platform and points to a footbridge. "Maybe we could jump on to the train as it passes through?"

"Sure. Ever done that before? Ever jumped off a high bridge onto a fast-moving train? No? I didn't think so. Because you'd be dead."

He turns away. "It was just an idea."

"This isn't the movies, Kieran."

"What do you suggest?"

I look around, forcing my brain into action. How are we going to get aboard the freight train? It's not going to slow down or stop just for us.

Or is it?

"Maybe one of us could stand on the track," I suggest, "so it has to stop. Then, the other one could sneak on."

Now it's his turn to rip my idea to shreds. "Brilliant, Zac. So, one of us has to get arrested.

And that's if the train doesn't run them down first. I think my plan was less risky than that."

"What about if it wasn't you or me?" I say.

"You're suggesting we kidnap someone and tie them to the tracks?"

"Don't be an idiot. I'm wondering if we can block the tracks with something. If there was an obstacle in the way, the train would have to stop."

"There was a level crossing further down," points out Kieran. "We could break into a car, release the handbrake, and push it over the tracks."

I think it through. "They'd know someone had done that on purpose and they'd probably figure out why. It has to look like an accident. Something that won't make them suspicious."

Kieran glances around. "A tree?"

There's no shortage of those.

"It could work," I admit. "But how would we do it? We're not lumberjacks."

"It wouldn't need to be massive." Kieran jumps off the end of the small platform and starts walking alongside the railway tracks. "It just has to look big enough to cause damage to the train."

I follow him as he wades through nettles,

checking the trees that are standing nearby. He pushes on a few, testing their strength.

"These are too solid," he concludes. "Let's keep going. There's bound to be a better one further down."

The further we go, the less likely it seems that his plan will work. Still, he presses on, examining the trees.

"Even if you find a thinner one, how will we get it down?" I ask.

"I have this." Kieran reaches into his camo trousers and pulls out a small knife. "It's hardly an axe, but if we cut through part of a trunk with it, it might be enough."

"I guess."

The first rays of sun appear when our luck changes.

Kieran walks over to a tree with a thin white trunk. "This one will do," he says. "It's pretty tall, but I reckon we could get it down."

"It's worth a try."

He takes out his knife and starts digging in to the bark.

"It's going to take a while," he says.

"I'll wait over here," I say, settling down on the

ground. "I'm shattered."

He ignores me, probably annoyed that I'm leaving him to do all the work. But I can't help it; I can barely keep my eyes open.

Lying there amongst the trees, the birds singing overhead, I can almost forget the stress we're under. It's hard to imagine millions of people will die if we fail. All of that seems like it's happening in a different world.

Right here, right now, the world is at peace.

Exhausted, I drift off to sleep.

NINE

Kieran kicks me. "Wake up, sleepyhead. I need your help."

I groan and sit up. "What time is it?"

He checks his watch. "Just gone ten. We don't have long. You've been asleep for hours."

"Only a few. I need another twelve at least."

"Well, maybe you can get some rest on the train. That's what I'm hoping to do."

"Making any progress?" I ask him, glancing over at the tree.

"Take a look."

I clamber to my feet and wander over. Kieran has whittled away at the trunk until he's more than halfway through.

"I don't have time to do much more, but I figure if we both push, the tree might come down."

"It's worth a shot. Besides, it's not like we have a backup plan."

He grins. "Come on, Zac. Since when did *we* ever have one of those?"

We try pushing and pulling. We're not worried it's going to collapse on us; too much of the trunk is still attached. Even if it snaps, the tree will come down slowly. At least, that's what we're hoping. Either way, this isn't the time for caution.

"You need to climb on that long branch," suggests Kieran.

"Why me?"

"Because one of us still needs to be pulling the trunk from here, and you're too weak."

It's half-insult, half-fact, but I don't object. Kieran gives me a leg up into one of the sturdier branches, and I cling on for dear life as he pulls hard on the damaged trunk.

"Jump up and down," he says.

"I'm not a monkey."

"Just do what you can. We don't have long."

He's right; we have to stop that train.

I bounce on the tree branch, while he renews

his efforts, tugging on the trunk. There's a cracking, splintering noise as something gives way. I feel the tree move beneath me and I almost fall.

As I cling to my perch, I can see the ground coming closer. But I manage to jump off and dive out of the way as the tree lands on its side.

I dust myself off. "You forgot to shout *timber*."

"Has anyone ever told you, you're an ungrateful little turd?" He pushes past. "Do you think it's blocking enough of the train tracks?"

"I'd say so." Only the very top of the tree reaches the railway line, but there are enough leaves and branches to block the train's path.

"So, what now?" he asks.

"We hide out nearby and jump on as soon as the train comes to a stop."

"If Howard's timings were right, we only have five minutes."

That sharpens our minds as we scout out the undergrowth. Thankfully, there are some thick bushes we can crouch behind.

"These should be far enough from the driver for us not to be seen," I say. "Besides, I'm hoping he's so distracted by the tree that he doesn't pay any attention to what's happening all the way back here."

"Let's hope so."

***

We hear it before we see it.

There's a faint rumbling sound. As the train draws closer, I feel a slight tremor in the ground, followed by the chunter of carriages.

Kieran and I are behind the bush, peeping out between the leaves.

"It's not going to stop," I say, my voice almost drowned out by the noise.

He frowns. "It has to."

The words are hardly out of his mouth when there's a loud squeal, the screech of metal on metal. The driver has seen the tree. Still, it won't be enough. He's too late; it takes a train about a mile to stop and he doesn't have anywhere near that distance. The train isn't going to stop; it's going to crash. I wonder why I didn't think of it before.

"He's going to hit it," I mutter.

We watch as the train rushes past our hiding

place, still going way too fast, the screeching getting louder.

"Come on," I urge Kieran. "We have to board now. While it's slowing down. He might not come to a complete stop."

Kieran nods and we emerge from behind the bush, running towards the moving carriages. I glance down the line. The front of the train is only metres from the tree. But there's a problem: the carriages are just big containers made of smooth corrugated metal.

"There's nothing to hold on to," says Kieran.

By now, the train has reached the tree. It's moving with enough force to smash the small branches to pieces and carry on.

Our obstacle was useless, just like our plan.

As the back of the train sweeps towards us, there's only one thing that gives me hope. The last wagon is a flatbed; a metal carriage without a container.

"We can get on that!" I dash forward, throwing myself on to the metal platform. I keep my legs clear of the wheels as I pull myself up. Then, I turn around and offer a hand to Kieran, who's still dangling from the side.

My heart thuds as we sit there, trees rushing past on either side. It might be my imagination, but I think the train is speeding up now the tree is no longer in the way.

"We might be on the train, but we're far from safe," I point out.

Kieran snorts. "There's that cheery optimism again."

"I just mean we'll be spotted if the train goes through a town or something. Or when it arrives at its destination. We have to find a better place to hide."

Kieran wanders over to the end of the flatbed. He balances precariously as he pulls a metal handle on the next wagon, trying to open the container. "They're locked. No way we can get inside."

"How about on top?" I suggest, looking up.

"Good idea."

Kieran uses the handholds to scramble up the side. He makes it look way too easy. Being in the Resistance, both of us have had to learn skills we never thought we'd need. He reaches down to help me do the same.

Once we're on top, we're no longer protected

from the wind. The air rushes past as the train thunders ahead. If we lie flat, we'll stay relatively well hidden.

"How long will it take us to get to the docks?" asks Kieran.

I shrug. "I don't know. I never asked."

"Brilliant as always, Zac," he teases. He lies down on his back, looking up at the sky. "You'd better keep a lookout. I might try to get some sleep."

"Fair." I guess I already got a few hours while he sawed the tree. Besides, I don't much like the idea of trying to rest up here. Even though the container roof is flat, I'd be too afraid of falling off.

Kieran opens one eye. "I don't suppose you have any idea what we're going to do when we get there? Or a plan for how we destroy the vaccine?"

I sigh and look away.

"I guessed not," he replies, "but I just thought I'd check."

TEN

I can smell the sea.

It brings back happy memories. I remember going to the beach as a kid, playing in the sand.

That was before the news started carrying stories about Vicron-X, way before the lockdown. How long has it been now? At least two years stuck at home followed by months working for the Resistance. I lose track.

I realise how much I've missed.

If we end the lockdown, maybe life could return to normal. I'd be happy to go back to a life of video games and family holidays. If I ever find my family.

I roll onto my side and prop myself up on my elbow. I have a great view from up here. There are hills on either side, but in front of us I glimpse the ocean. It won't be long before we reach the docks.

Kieran is fast asleep, but I nudge him awake.

"I think we're nearly there."

He sits up and rubs his eyes. "What I wouldn't give for another hour's sleep."

"Tell me about it."

He looks around, admiring the view. "Is that the sea?"

"Sure is." The train sweeps around a bend and I see a tunnel straight ahead. "Kieran, get down." He's being slow, so I dive on top of him, forcing him flat on the train's roof.

"Hey, bro, what gives?"

I don't need to answer, because a second later we're inside the tunnel. If Kieran had been sitting up, he'd have lost his head.

When we emerge and scramble upright, Kieran's eyes are wide. He tries to keep his cool. "I suppose you want me to thank you?"

I put my hands behind my head, looking smug. "That would be nice."

"Well, it's not going to happen." Kieran gives me a playful kick. "I've saved your sorry butt enough times."

That's true. He has.

I can see tall metal towers rising in the distance. "The docks, I'm guessing."

"Now would be a great time to come up with some sort of plan," suggests Kieran, "or we could just bounce from one disaster to another, like usual."

"That *is* the plan," I joke. I only wish it weren't true. Reaching the docks is a good start, but once we're there, surrounded by containers full of the poisoned vaccine, how do we even begin to destroy it all? "I don't suppose you're carrying a bomb?"

"Yeah, sure," he replies, giving me a withering look. "I keep one in my pants."

The train is drawing closer now and we can see the dockyard up ahead. A huge cargo ship is being loaded with steel containers. Even though each one is the size of a lorry, the cranes are lifting them through the air and lowering them to the deck with ease. It looks like someone is playing with a massive Lego set.

Workers in orange virus protection suits are busy on the dockyard, attaching hooks and directing the drivers of the cranes.

"It looks like the vaccine might already be on the cargo ship," I mutter, "and there's no way to get on board without being seen."

"There's a lot of people down there," agrees Kieran. "So, what do we do?"

The train slows down as it pulls into the dockyard.

"We can't stay up here. They'll unload these containers and we'll get squashed by a crane or caught by one of the workers. We have to get down." I peer over the edge of the train that faces away from the dockyard. On this side, there's nothing. A deserted stretch of land leads to a chain-link fence. "It's a long way down."

"You're such a flake," says Kieran. He's already lowering his body over the side. In one smooth movement, he twists and lets go, landing like a gymnast on the dirt. He stands up and dusts himself off. "Your turn."

I pull a face. "I can't drop that far. I'll break my legs."

"I'll catch you."

I'm not keen on the idea, but I can hear workers approaching the train from the other side. If I hang around any longer, I'll get caught.

I swing my body around and ease my lower half off the edge.

Kieran is standing below, looking as nervous as me.

"You sure about this?" I hiss at him.

"Just get it done, before I change my mind."

I force myself further back, wondering if I'll be brave enough to let go. As it happens, I don't need to work up the courage to do it, because gravity takes over. There isn't much to hold on to on top of the container and my body slips back without warning. Then, I'm falling through the air, my heart in my throat.

I land on Kieran like a sack of potatoes, knocking him to the ground. As I jump up, he lets out a groan.

"Are you okay?" I ask.

"You weigh a lot for a skinny runt."

I help him up. "I think we head to the front of the train, before all the containers are lifted off."

"Makes sense."

We sneak forwards, darting between the carriages, aware that workers are on the other side. Thankfully, the virus protection suits rustle loudly and limit their vision, so they don't spot us sneaking between the wagons. We reach the front without much difficulty.

We peer out at the dockyard.

It's massive. When I set out to come here, I hadn't thought it through. Now, I'm faced with an impossible task.

"So, those containers all have the vaccine in?" asks Kieran.

"Some of them," I reply. "I'm guessing the red ones with 'Bird Laboratories' on the side."

"Zac, there must be at least fifty of them. We don't know how many more are already on the ship. And that number is growing by the minute."

I bite my lip, thinking hard. "Maybe that's a good thing."

Now Kieran's confused. "I thought we were trying to stop them?"

"We are. But it might be easier to destroy the vaccine when it's on board. We could sink the ship."

He gives me one of his looks. "You know I was joking about having a bomb in my pants, right?"

"Hear me out. We sneak on board, wait until the ship is at sea, then take the pilot hostage and make him crash. If it sinks, all the vaccine is ruined and none of it gets taken anywhere."

Kieran does not look impressed. "That's the craziest plan I've ever heard."

"Have you got anything better?"

"No," he admits.

"In that case, let's move."

ELEVEN

We move closer to the ship, sneaking between rows of containers.

"Maybe we should get inside one of these," suggests Kieran. "It doesn't look like they're checking the contents. It might be the easiest way on board."

I consider it for a moment. "I'm not sure you can open them from inside. We might get trapped."

He peers at the dockside. "Well, unless you have an invisibility cloak, we're never going to get past all those guys without being seen. However busy they are, they'd notice us running over the gangway on to the ship."

I watch them for a few minutes, trying to discern the rhythm of their activity. Most of them are helping to direct the cranes to pick up the containers, but a few are carrying smaller items on board.

I clutch Kieran's jacket. "That's it," I hiss. "We don't sneak past. We walk past."

He gives me another of his looks. "Brilliant," he says. "Why didn't I think of that?"

"Listen," I urge him. "We just need virus protection suits. Once we've got those on, everyone will think we work here. Then, we can walk on to the ship with boxes and no one will be any the wiser."

"It might work," he allows. "But where are you planning to get them from?"

I glance around. There's a large brick building in the middle of the dockyard. "That must be where the workers get changed and go to the toilet. I reckon if there's any spare suits, they'll be in there."

"Won't there also be more workers?" he asks.

"Maybe. That's why we'll be quiet."

He shakes his head. "One day, you're going to get us caught. Or killed."

I grin at him. "You missed me when I was in Arcadia. Admit it."

"Maybe a little."

We steal towards the building, making a mad dash for the back door as soon as we're sure the coast is clear. Thankfully, it's not locked. A narrow hallway leads to some toilets and showers, next to a changing room. Kieran forces open a locker with his knife. He curses when he sees that it's empty.

"What if there aren't any spares?" he asks.

"There must be," I insist. "This is a huge operation. They need replacement suits in case one gets ripped."

"They wouldn't keep those in here," points out Kieran. "These lockers are for personal belongings."

"Let's check upstairs."

We creep up a narrow staircase. At the top is a short corridor. One door is open. It leads to a large recreation room with torn chairs and a dirty-looking kitchenette. I doubt anyone has used that for years; no one is allowed to socialise with the virus on the loose, and it wouldn't be much fun sitting around in one of the cumbersome suits.

Kieran gestures at the closed doors. We're

going to have to open one of them if we want to carry on hunting. I nod and point at the one on the right. He reaches down and turns the handle.

Another empty room. This one has a first aid station with a thin bed. Kieran checks in a cupboard.

"You were right, bro," he says, pulling out an orange virus protection suit. "They do keep a spare."

"I'm always right," I remind him. "Is there more than one?"

"They've got a few in here. None for a midget like you, though."

"I'll manage."

We tug on the suits. Mine is so baggy I can barely keep it on my shoulders. Kieran places the helmet over my head.

"Bro, you look ridiculous. That's worse than your skintight stuff."

I should be offended, but he's right. I'm wondering if the plan will work. Kieran is a year older and much bigger than me, halfway between boy and man. With the helmet on, he could pass as an adult. I'm never going to look like anything but a kid in fancy dress.

"They're going to know I'm not a dock worker."

"Only if they get close. We might still pull it off, if we keep our distance."

We trudge down the stairs.

I'm tense as we approach the back door. Are we really going to do this? Do we have any hope of sneaking past the workers on the dock?

The nerves get the better of me and I tug on Kieran's shoulder. "Wait. I need the toilet."

He sighs. "You've got to be kidding."

"My stomach's in knots. I need to go."

"Be quick."

I dash into one of the empty cubicles and pull down the suit. I almost don't make it in time. I'm just cleaning up when I hear Kieran hissing at me through the cubicle door.

"Someone's coming. Stay where you are. Don't say anything."

He disappears, or at least I think he does. It's hard to tell what's going on.

Heavy footsteps approach and someone steps into the cubicle next to mine, slamming the door. He whistles as he sits down.

I gulp and unlock my cubicle.

The man speaks. "Frank, is that you?"

I make a non-committal grunt, then dash for the exit. If I stay in here any longer, the man might figure out something suspicious is going on.

Kieran is waiting in the corridor, looking nervous. "Let's get out of here," he murmurs. "No more toilet breaks."

"Agreed."

TWELVE

We approach the dockside.

My breath steams up the visor, making it hard to see.

I guess we could just stroll towards the ship, now that we're dressed like the other guys, but I can barely walk in the baggy suit, and I know I look way too small to be working here. We don't want to come out into the open until we have to.

"What we really need is a distraction," I say. "That way, people are less likely to be watching when we go on board."

"Got any ideas?"

I glance around. At this end of the yard there are stacks of shipping containers and an abandoned forklift truck. "Do you remember the ambulance at the medical facility?"

"Yeah, sure."

"I reckon we could do the same with that." I point at the forklift.

Kieran grins. "You really like crashing things, don't you?"

Back when I was working for the Resistance, before I went undercover in Arcadia, the two of us had been asked to spy on a quarantine facility. Kieran got too close and was caught. I was only able to rescue him by crashing an ambulance to create a diversion.

"It needs to look like a malfunction," I point out, "or they'll get suspicious."

"Send it off the dockside. That'll create one hell of a splash."

I creep over to the truck. The controls look simple enough. They've even left a key in the ignition.

"As soon as I get this moving, we head over to the ship," I tell him.

I climb in and turn the key, wondering if the sound will attract any attention, but we're hidden by a row of containers. Heavy machinery is at work around us, lifting and stacking the cargo. That means I have a few moments to experiment, finding the pedal that makes the forklift crawl forwards.

"What are you waiting for?" hisses Kieran. "Let's go."

"I need something to hold down this pedal," I say. "Otherwise, the moment I take my foot off, it stops."

He frowns and starts hunting around. Eventually, he hands me a brick. "Will this do?"

"It's perfect."

I take a deep breath and grip the steering wheel. It's now or never.

The vehicle starts moving, and I set my sights on the dockside. If I get this right, the forklift will drive right past the men and over the edge into the sea below.

I only have seconds to plant the brick and get out of here. It's harder than I think to get it to balance, but somehow I manage it. As I land on the ground, I trip over the baggy material of the suit, my body slamming into the tarmac. Thankfully, no one sees. I'm back behind the container in no time, Kieran next to me.

"Watch out!" shouts one worker. "That forklift's gone haywire!"

"Now's our chance," hisses Kieran.

As we slip out from our hiding place, no one is paying any attention. A few of the workers are running towards the forklift, hoping to reach it before it goes over the edge.

We hurry over the gangway. As soon as we're aboard the ship, we hear a splash and more shouting. The forklift made it to the water. We sidle between the stacked containers, looking for the best place to hide. There are narrow gaps between each row of the metal boxes, just big enough to walk down.

"I guess we could hide between two rows," suggests Kieran.

"If anyone walks past either end, they'll see us."

"Got any other ideas?"

I hate that. He always expects me to come up with all the answers. We haven't seen any decent hiding places, and he knows it. I might be the brains of the operation, but I'm tired and my head aches.

"It would be better to get on top of the containers. Like we did on the train."

Kieran glances up. "That was just one. These

are in stacks of four."

"You think I don't know that?"

"Well, unless you've got a really big ladder, it's not possible."

I swear and turn away.

It's not our first spat, and it won't be our last. When you're always a hair's breadth from being caught and carted off into quarantine or prison, the stress is intense.

As I lean against the massive wall of containers, I assess the situation. We can't stay here. Someone is bound to see us, and there's nowhere to run if they do. There are two exits, one at either end, and it's much too easy to block them both.

I can feel the corrugated metal through the thin plastic of the virus protection suit. It's cold and hard, like the bars of a cage.

Then, it comes to me. A flash of inspiration.

I place one foot on the wall of steel opposite and push hard. Then I do the same with my other foot. Now, I can inch my way up the gap in the containers, my back on one wall and my feet on the other.

"Hey, bro," I say. "I think we can get up. Copy

me."

Kieran turns around and sees me a few metres off the ground. "That's genius."

My legs are already feeling the strain. "It's not easy, though. We could slip and fall near the top."

"We're much too pro for that," he jokes. He follows my example, edging his body up the narrow gap.

We take it slow. Still, there's a terrifying moment when my foot slips. For a second, I think I've miscalculated and that I'm going to fall. Now I'm at least five metres in the air, I'd break a few bones for sure, maybe even my neck.

Somehow, I keep myself in place with my other foot while I scramble for purchase on the container opposite. The top is a few metres away and I don't know how long I can keep this up. I'm beginning to think the whole idea was a huge mistake.

Then, just when I think things can't get any worse, they do.

"Quiet," hisses Kieran. "Someone's coming."

THIRTEEN

We freeze, our tired legs holding us in place. My muscles strain with the effort. If I hold this position for too long, I'll get cramp. From the look on Kieran's face, he's feeling the same, but there's nothing we can do but wait it out.

We hear conversation, the casual banter of workmates. Then, we see them. Two men in protective clothing walk past the end of the row. One of them glances down the gap as they pass, but he doesn't look up. If we'd stayed down there, we'd have been seen. As it is, we're safe.

Well, as safe as you can be when you're several metres in the air with no harness.

The conversation fades as the men get further away.

Kieran and I exchange looks. We have to get to

the top before they come back, and before our legs give out.

We shuffle up, little by little.

When we reach the top, it's a mad scramble to pull ourselves up and on to the roof of the stack. Kieran manages it first, then gives me a hand. We lie on our backs, panting. My whole body is shaking.

"That was too close," I whisper.

Kieran is less worried. "We made it. That's what matters."

He's right, but one day our luck will run out.

Not today.

We have a mission to complete. If we don't destroy the vaccine, millions of people will die. I'm used to the stakes being high, but I can't get my head around those kinds of numbers. And two of those people are my mum and my brother, Joe. I have to do this for them.

It's a good hiding place. A few cranes tower above us on the dockside, but no one operating them can see us. The only place higher than us is the bridge, which sticks up halfway down the ship. I can only hope that as we're at the back of the boat, the pilot is facing the other way.

"What now?" asks Kieran.

There it is again: him expecting me to have the answers.

"We wait until we're a short way out at sea. Then, we make our way to the cockpit and take the pilot hostage so we can make him crash."

"How? We could travel for miles without seeing another boat."

"We'll make him turn it around and head towards land. There are cliffs a short distance from here. We passed them on the train."

Kieran leans on his elbow as he looks at me. "What happens to us?"

"You can swim, right?"

He snorts and lies back down. "That's what I thought."

***

It takes an age for the ship to leave.

Kieran and I are lying on our backs in the sun, the sea-breeze keeping us cool. It would be relaxing if it weren't for the need for constant vigilance. Instead, we're both edgy and nervous, wondering if we'll succeed. We've stripped off the orange protective suits and visors. There's no way we want to stay in those any longer than we have to, and there's no legitimate reason for workers to be up here.

There's more shouting than normal as the men make the final preparations. We feel the vibrations as the massive engine starts up. Until now, the gentle movement of the sea has been hardly noticeable. Now we've left dock, we can feel the ship rise and fall on the waves. They get bigger as we move further from shore.

"How long do we leave it?" asks Kieran, lying on his side so he can watch the dock recede into the distance.

"Just far enough so we can't be seen. A couple more minutes."

We wait it out, ensuring that we won't be visible from land. The last thing we need is someone spotting us from the dockside and raising the alarm before we've had a chance to get to the cockpit.

I pull myself up and crawl over to the edge of the container, acutely aware of the steep drop to the deck. "I'm not sure how we get down."

"I don't think we need to." Kieran's crouched

behind me, looking towards the other stacks. "We can jump the gaps, from one roof to another, until we get close to the bridge. Then we can reach that staircase."

"Won't someone see us?"

"We're as safe up here as we would be on deck."

I don't like the idea of jumping between the containers. I look at the one across from us. I know I can make that distance, but somehow being so high up makes it feel harder.

"Let's get going." Kieran takes a running jump, crossing the gap with ease and landing on the other side.

I step back from the edge.

"Come on, Zac," urges Kieran.

My throat feels tight and I swallow hard. There's no way out of this. Even if I don't jump, I have to find a way down. That's even more scary.

I force my legs into action, trying to imagine that I'm just trying to clear a puddle. I don't want to think about the drop.

Somehow, it works, and I easily clear the distance. That gives me confidence for the next jump. And the next.

Before I know it, we've jumped several rows and are standing on the last line of cargo. Across from us is the central tower, which leads to the bridge. There's a balcony with a railing, but it's further than everything we've jumped so far.

"You reckon we can make it?" asks Kieran.

"I don't want to try," I admit. "We'll end up splattered on the deck."

"I'm not sure we have any other option."

Kieran takes a few steps back, to give himself the most running distance he can manage. "Here goes nothing." He runs and launches himself into the air, slamming into the railings of the balcony opposite. He grips them for dear life, then gets a foothold and climbs over. "Easy. Your turn."

I peer over the edge. The deck looks so far down. "I can't do this."

"Sure you can."

When I look back at Kieran, though, the jump is the last of my worries.

Standing right behind him is a man in an orange suit.

FOURTEEN

The man grabs Kieran by the arm. "What do you boys think you're playing at?"

"Let go." Kieran struggles to get free. He pushes the man hard, knocking him back.

His attacker regains his balance and lunges forward, this time forcing Kieran to the ground. Within seconds, he has him in an armlock, his face pressed against the metal gantry.

"Get off me," cries Kieran.

"No chance. You shouldn't be here." The man pulls a radio from his pocket. "I've caught an intruder on the landing below the cockpit. There's another boy on top of the containers. I've got one of them but I'm requesting support to catch the other."

If I don't want every person on this ship

coming after me, I have to give them something else to do. Without thinking, I lean over the side of the container and shout down. "Lads, they're on to us. Run and hide, all of you!"

There's no one down there, of course, but they don't know that.

Sure enough, Kieran's attacker is taken in by my ruse. "There are more of them, down on the deck. Search the ship and I'll keep my eye on these two."

He might be able to watch me, but he can't move from his current position without letting Kieran go. I have to act now, before he realises I was lying about having friends below. I launch myself off the top of the container, sail through the air and smash into the railing. The force knocks me back and my feet slip. I cling for dear life to the metal bars, my legs swinging below the gantry.

Kieran attempts to distract his captor. He rolls to the side, throwing him off balance, then tries to push his body off the floor. The man is having none of it; he has much too tight a grip. But that was never the point. For a few critical seconds, the guy has been focusing on Kieran, not me. In that time, I've somehow pulled myself up and over the railing and I'm standing on the balcony next to them.

I may not be as strong as either Kieran or his attacker, but both my hands are free. The man is wearing an orange hood with a visor. I grab it with both hands from behind and spin it round so he can't see. He pulls away from me, reaching up to take hold of it, but while he does it, Kieran slips away from his grasp. By the time he's twisted his visor around, he finds Kieran is holding a knife to his neck.

"Don't make me use this," warns Kieran. "One wrong move and I'll slit your throat. Do you understand?" Kieran uses a different voice when he's threatening people. I don't like it, but it works. I wonder if I'll ever sound as cold as him. I hope not.

The man nods.

Kieran stands behind him, pushing him forwards. "Give me your radio and take us to the bridge."

Our prisoner hands it over and leads us up a couple of flights of stairs to the very top of the ship. Here, a flat balcony leads to a white metal door.

"Open it," demands Kieran.

The man reaches up and turns the handle. Kieran pushes him inside.

It's a large room full of control panels. Above them is a line of windows, giving a clear view over the top of the containers to the ocean beyond. Good job we were hiding at the back of the ship or we'd have been spotted for sure.

A pilot is facing away from us, his eyes on the horizon, but he swivels around as we enter. His eyes go wide when he sees us holding a knife to his colleague's throat. "Aren't you a little young to be pirates?"

"We're not pirates," insists Kieran. "We're the Resistance. And unless you do what we say, your mate is going to end up without his head."

The pilot tries to act casual. He half-swivels back to his console. "Calm down, lad. What exactly are you after?"

I run over and grab his hand, which was subtly heading for a hidden panic button. "You can leave that alone for a start. Try to press that again, and your colleague dies. Got it?"

He nods, his face pale.

"Now, turn this ship around. Head for the cliffs."

"The cliffs?" The man's forehead creases. "How close do you plan to get?"

"We're going for a head-on collision."

"But you'll sink us," objects the pilot.

"Now you're getting it."

"Do as he says," demands Kieran. "Or I'll kill your friend. Then I'll kill you. And don't even think about trying to contact anyone. Only if you do everything we say will you get out of this alive."

"It'll take some time," he warns us. "A ship this size has a large turning circle."

"We understand that," I assure him.

The pilot gets to work, flipping switches. We feel the boat straining as he changes course.

"Ok. We're heading for the cliffs. But why do you want to sink us?" asks the pilot. "We're carrying the vaccine abroad. Surely that's something the Resistance support? Soon, the lockdown will be over."

"The vaccine isn't safe," I tell him. I don't see any reason to conceal the truth. "We have to destroy it."

His colleague interrupts. "You boys have been listening to too many conspiracy theories. Why would anyone poison the vaccine?"

I can't be bothered to explain. "How many people are on this ship?"

"Twelve, including us."

"Are you sure?"

"It's a skeleton crew."

"It will be, if you don't do as you're told," growls Kieran. That's a little unnecessary given that the men are following our instructions to the letter.

I turn back to the pilot. "You must have a liferaft, I'm guessing?"

"Of course. More than one."

"Tell the others to abandon ship. Give them a direct order."

"What about us?" asks the man who has the knife to his throat.

"Once we're on course for the cliff, we'll let you jump overboard," I tell him. "You can swim to shore."

"You know you'll never get away with this?" asks the pilot.

I can't help wondering if he's right.

***

The cliffs tower in the distance.

The ship is powering towards them, the relentless pull of its massive engine moving us closer to inevitable disaster. I'm not sure we could turn around now, even if we wanted.

A short while ago, we watched the liferaft leave. I counted ten people on board, but we have no way of knowing if the pilot was telling the truth about the size of the crew.

"Ok," I say, "it's time to abandon ship. Leave the engines on full power. Let's go downstairs."

The men do as they're told. We traipse down several sets of stairs, over to a rusted white railing at the edge of the deck.

"Can we at least take off our protective suits?" asks the pilot. "No one can swim in this gear."

"One at a time, but be quick. Don't try anything."

The man pulls off his hood and then unzips his protective suit so he can step out. Then, Kieran switches the knife to the pilot's throat while his colleague strips off his gear.

"Over the side," I demand.

The men climb over the railing.

"I sure hope you boys know what you're doing," says the pilot.

"I sure hope you guys can swim," retorts Kieran. "Time to go, gentlemen."

The pilot looks at his colleague and shrugs. He lets go of the railing and dives into the ocean. His colleague follows close behind.

"Do you think they were lying about the number of people on board?" I ask.

Kieran glances towards the front of the ship. "It doesn't matter. No one can stop us crashing now. Let's get out of here."

"Agreed."

We clamber over the railings, the cliffs looming above us. We're going to hit them any second now.

"I hope we haven't left this too late," mutters Kieran.

"Just shut up and jump."

FIFTEEN

It's like hitting a sheet of ice.

As I plunge under the freezing water, I struggle to hold my breath, the cold knocking the air from my lungs. I force myself to stay calm as I swim away from the hull of the ship. I need to get as far as I can; I don't want to be caught in the propellers.

When I break the surface, I gasp for breath and check my position. I'm still much too close to the vessel. Kieran bobs up a short distance away.

"Come on, Zac," he urges, turning towards the shore. "This is no time to admire the scenery."

I'd answer him back, but I'm too out of breath to speak, so I just do as I'm told, trying my best to keep up as he swims further away.

There's an earth-shattering noise as the ship

slams into the cliff. I can feel the vibrations through the water. Everything seems to happen more slowly than it should. There's the screeching of metal. Then, a crack, as if the earth is being ripped in two. A huge chunk of rock falls forward on to the deck. It rocks the boat like it's a toy.

That causes a massive swell of water which sweeps towards us, lifting us into the air and then plunging us back down beneath the waves. When I resurface, it's total chaos. The ferry is lying partly on its side, most of the containers falling into the water; the others teetering on the edge. Rocks continue to fall from above, the cliff cracked and unstable.

"Satisfied?" teases Kieran, bobbing behind me in the water.

"It'll do," I pant.

"It'll attract attention," he points out. "We'd better get out of here."

We swim along the coast. The water's not getting any warmer and I'm shattered. I'm beginning to think that we'll drown when we round a headland and spot an inlet. I use the last of my energy to pull my body towards it.

As I scramble onto the slippery rocks, waves push past, making me lose my balance. I stumble along until I'm beyond the reach of the sea. Then, I collapse on top of a large boulder, trying to catch my breath.

Kieran's already on his feet, checking our surroundings. "There's no path, but the cliff is less steep here. I think we could climb up."

My legs are still trembling. "I can't. I'm too exhausted."

He shakes his head. "You don't have a choice. We have to get out of here."

"I need some time to recover."

"A couple of minutes. No more."

***

Kieran is relentless.

Two minutes have barely gone by before he's dragging me to my feet and pointing out our route.

"It looks pretty steep," I tell him. "What if we fall?"

"We die," he says. "So, let's make sure we don't."

"That's great. Really great."

Kieran leads the way, clambering up a pile of rocks. I follow close behind, trying not to look at the near-vertical slope towering above us. I'm thankful that the active wear from Arcadia is already warming up and drying out. Kieran is nowhere near as lucky; his army gear is still dripping.

"I suggest you don't look down," he says, as he begins the more challenging part of the climb, scaling the rock-face with no rope.

"I'll bear that in mind."

"Cheer up, bro. We'll soon be at the top."

I reach for the first hand-hold. "I hope so."

I'm out of breath before I've started, and I sound like an old man as I puff and pant my way up the cliff. I reach and pull, every manoeuvre causing me pain. I can't think about anything. My entire focus is on the next move, the next step. I zone out, surrendering myself to exhilaration and fear.

"There's a tricky bit here," warns Kieran. "Not much to hold on to."

His words jar me out of my reverie. I glance up to see him stretching towards a tiny crack.

Somehow, he digs his fingers in and hauls his body up another few feet. From there, he drags himself on to a small ledge to safety.

I try to do the same, but I'm much shorter than he is; I'm a year younger and I've always been small for my age. There's no way I can reach.

"It's no good. I can't do it," I say.

I glance up at Kieran, wondering if he's mad. Instead, I see him pulling off his camo shirt.

He lowers it towards me. "Hold on to this. I'll pull you."

I gulp and look down. Big mistake. I hadn't realised how far we'd come. "I can't."

"If you don't, I'll push you off this cliff myself."

It's not a serious threat. I know that. He's joking. Not that it's funny. But he snaps me out of my cowardice. It's not like I have options. I reach out and grab the wet shirt, wrapping the sleeve around my hand.

"Ready?" asks Kieran.

"As ready as I'll ever be."

"Ok, on three. One... two... THREE." Kieran pulls the shirt towards him and I step out onto a jutting rock, which is just enough to help me past the smooth rock-face and up onto the ledge where he's sitting. I almost fall on top of him, my heart thudding.

"See? Easy!" he says, clapping me on the shoulder. But he looks as relieved as I feel.

"How much further?" I ask, almost afraid to glance up.

"Not far," he assures me.

I wonder if he's lying to keep my spirits up, but just a short climb later, it becomes a lot less steep. We can almost stand up for the last part. Even though I'm exhausted, the joy of seeing our destination is enough to carry me the rest of the way.

By the time we scramble to the top, Kieran bundles me into the tall grass, laughing.

"We did it! We destroyed the vaccine and made it out alive!"

I push him off and lie on the ground, my limbs stretched out in the sun. "As long as they can't retrieve any of those containers."

"From the bottom of the cliff? Even if any of them survived, they're way out of reach."

"I guess."

"So, what do we do now?" he asks.

"I want to sleep for a week," I say, closing my

eyes.

"I don't think that's a good idea," says Kieran.

"Why not?"

"Because someone's coming."

I sit up. Kieran's right. I can hear rustling in the bushes.

Why can't everyone just leave us alone?

Kieran pulls me to my feet, and we try to run.

I say 'try' because I'm so shattered, I can barely walk. I limp along like an old man, wincing with every step. We at least make it into a maze of shrubs where we can't be seen, but if they have anything that tracks body heat, then we're done for.

"Go on without me," I urge Kieran.

"No way, bro. We stand or fall together." He glances back, standing on tiptoe so he can see over the bushes.

"Is it the Quarantine Agency or the police?"

"Does it matter?"

He has a point. Either is bad news.

Kieran pulls me on, deeper into the undergrowth. We push our way between the branches. As we emerge into a clearing, we find ourselves face to face with the man we fought on the ship. He does not look happy.

"Well, look who it is," he drawls. "I said you wouldn't get far."

Kieran reaches down to his ankle, but when he brings his hand up, it's empty. "Zac, I lost the knife."

"Not so cocky without a weapon, eh?" The man moves towards us, his face a picture of hate. "I'm gonna enjoy handing you boys over to the police, after I've taken some revenge of my own."

"Zac, run," says Kieran. "I'll catch you up."

I feel guilty doing that when he just promised to stick by me, but if I don't get a head start, I'll just slow him down. I turn and limp back to the trees, glancing behind me as I go. The man lunges towards Kieran, a crazy look in his eyes. He's mad that we sank his boat, and he's going to make us pay.

Kieran isn't slow. He dodges out the way and trips the guy up.

"We don't have to fight," he says. "We can just go our separate ways."

"You'd like that, wouldn't you?" The man is back on his feet and lumbering towards Kieran again. His hands are bunched into fists and he swings wildly at his target.

Kieran moves quick. As if out of nowhere, he launches a roundhouse kick to the man's head, knocking him to the ground. Then, he jogs after me before the man has a chance to recover.

"Impressive," I grunt, as we run through the bushes. "Where did you learn to do that?"

"Cypher's men taught me some moves."

Our bid for freedom doesn't last long. The overgrown path leads us back to the clifftop where we started. But now someone else is standing there. A figure dressed in a black virus protection suit from head to foot. Sun glints off his visor, making it impossible to see his face.

I back towards the trees. "I don't suppose you can knock this guy out as well?"

"I doubt it," mutters Kieran. "He's got some kind of gun."

As he says it, the man raises his weapon and points it at me.

I turn and bolt for cover.

Seconds later, I feel it. Something slams into my back.

For a terrible few seconds, I wonder if I've been shot.

But it's not a bullet.

It's a tranquilliser dart.

I know because my legs turn to jelly and I collapse on the ground.

Then, the world goes black.

SIXTEEN

Everything hurts.

It's like I've been kicked repeatedly in the head. Maybe I have.

As I open my eyes, I'm expecting to see the cold grey walls of a quarantine cell, but I can make out blurry colourful shapes. As I focus, I discover it's dinosaur wallpaper. I groan as I roll over, taking in the rest of the surroundings. A desk piled high with toys. A floor covered in Lego. A wardrobe with a broken door. This isn't a cell; it's a little kid's bedroom.

That's not the only thing that's strange. I'm not handcuffed or restrained. The window is wide open; a gentle breeze ruffles the curtains. I wonder if I should try to escape before anyone realises I'm awake.

But, no.

I couldn't if I wanted to.

My body is a wreck.

And there's another thing; I glance under the covers and discover I'm naked.

I'm not going anywhere like this.

A small face appears at the doorway. The little eyes go wide when they see I'm conscious.

"He'th awake! He'th awake!"

There goes the element of surprise.

I hear the murmur of adult voices. Then, a middle-aged woman steps into the room. She has long brown hair and a warm smile.

"Morning, Zac." She reaches down and places the back of her hand on my forehead, checking my temperature. "How do you feel?"

"Like I've been hit by a bus."

"Most of that is down to the after-effects of the tranquilliser dart. Give it a few hours and your head will clear."

"Where am I?" I ask. "Am I a prisoner?"

"Thith ith my room," says the little boy, appearing from behind his mum. "Do you like it?"

I smile at him. Whatever is happening here,

he's not to blame. "I love it."

"I'm Danny," he says.

"I'm Zac."

"And I'm Maria, Danny's mum. You're not a prisoner, Zac. We're in the Resistance. They sent us to fetch you before you got arrested."

"They?" I ask, wondering which branch of the Resistance gave them the orders. If we're about to be handed back to Cypher, we're in trouble.

"Layla."

I relax a little. "What about Kieran?"

"He's downstairs, having breakfast."

"Typical," I mutter.

That makes her laugh. "There's some for you as well, when you feel ready. Or I could bring it up here if you like?"

"I don't have any clothes," I point out.

"They were wet and we had to make sure you didn't get hypothermia. My husband, Jake, got you some new things. I'll fetch them for you."

She disappears from the room, leaving me alone with Danny.

"Do you like dinosaurth?" he asks.

"Love them."

"Thith ith my T-Rex," he says, holding up one

of his toys. "Ith the biggetht."

"That is *scary*," I say, taking it from him and examining it. I hold it up and make a roaring noise. He giggles with glee.

Maria reappears with a stack of clothes in her arms. "I hope these fit." She places them on the end of the bed. "Come on, Danny. Leave Zac in peace. He needs to get dressed."

Reluctantly, Danny allows himself to be led out of the room. Just before he disappears, he smiles at me and I wink at him.

I sit up, ignoring my aching muscles. I feel a little dizzy, but I don't want to stay in bed any longer. Not until I've checked out my surroundings.

The clothes aren't like the army gear we wore when we lived at the pub. Instead, there are tight blue jeans and a black T-shirt with a white abstract design on it. There's also a stylish hoodie, some tight grey boxers and some white socks. They're the clothes teenagers are meant to wear, the sort of thing everyone had before the lockdown.

As I hold them, tears run down my cheeks.

I don't know why I'm being so sentimental

about stupid clothes. But somehow, this sample of normal life reminds me of everything I've lost and everything I've been through.

It's been so long since I was just a teenager.

I've lost so much of my life.

Snap out of it, Zac.

This isn't helping. I need to stay positive. I'm safe and warm and dry. There's food waiting for me downstairs.

I get dressed, enjoying the feel of the clothes on my skin.

Then, I look out the window. There's a large front garden with a driveway that leads on to a country lane. And trees. Lots of trees. I can't see any other houses, or any sign of a village. Just the woods. I can see why it's a good place for members of the Resistance to live. No one will see anyone coming or going from here.

My head feels a little fuzzy and I grip the banister as I make my way downstairs, following the smell of bacon.

I stumble into the large kitchen-diner. A man is cooking. He's young and fit, the sort of guy who could coach a football team, but he's also wearing a pink apron.

Behind him, Kieran sits at the breakfast bar, stuffing his face. He looks different to normal, and it takes a while for me to figure out why; he's no longer dressed like a reject from a punk band.

"He's alive!" he jokes, as he sees me walk in.

"Take a seat, Zac," says the man; Jake, I'm assuming. "You must be hungry."

I pull out a stool and perch next to Kieran. "Starving."

"Tough week, huh?" The man dishes up the food. "Do you like eggs?"

"Yeah, sure. Thanks."

"Dig in." He slides a plate in front of me. "You need some skin on those bones. You're light as a feather."

The comment catches me off guard.

How does he know how much I weigh?

But, then, I realise. This is the guy who shot me with a tranquilliser dart. He must have carried me back to his vehicle. And either he or his wife stripped me naked.

He seems to know what I'm thinking. "I'm sorry I had to shoot you, but you were like scared rabbits out there. I couldn't catch you and I didn't have time to explain."

I grunt, my mouth full.

"That area was crawling with police. You boys created quite a stir by crashing that ship. It was all over the news."

I pause, the bacon halfway to my mouth. "They know it was us?"

He laughs. "*They* don't. No. According to the news, no one knows what caused the crash, but they're guessing the Resistance are behind it. Layla told us it was you."

"Was she mad?" asks Kieran. He's thinking the same as me, wondering if we're in trouble.

Jake looks uneasy. "I don't think so, but she wants to talk to you. We'll set up a video link as soon as you're done with breakfast."

I nod and carry on eating.

Well, this will be fun.

SEVENTEEN

The screen flickers to life.

It's her.

Layla.

She'd have made a great supermodel with her angular features, slim features and smooth black skin.

"Zac? Kieran? What the hell have you boys been up to? Do you know how much trouble you're in?"

I'm getting some idea, yeah.

"It's Zac," says Kieran. "He's a bad influence."

This is no time for jokes.

I cut in, before Layla gets even more annoyed. "I sent you a message. The vaccine was poisoned. We had to destroy it."

Layla peers at me through the screen. "Cypher

says you've been compromised. He thinks the Collective are using you."

"He's wrong," I insist.

"Cypher isn't usually wrong. He's part AI."

"He's a nutter," mutters Kieran.

"He's higher up the chain of command than I am," snaps Layla. "We can't just ignore him."

"He's still wrong." I almost whisper it, worried I'll rile her even more. "You have to believe me. The vaccine is lethal. It'll kill everyone."

"You're sure about this?"

"Deadly. Those vaccine shots have been infected with a new strain of Vicron-X, or something worse. They won't just kill the people who get them, they'll infect everyone else."

"But why, Zac? Why would the Collective do that?" demands Layla.

"They want to wipe everyone out, to prevent climate change."

Layla rubs her eyes. She looks tired. "You really believe this?"

I lean closer to the screen. "I know it."

"If that's true, then we need to prevent the rest of it being distributed. You destroyed the main shipment that was being taken abroad. But the rest is being stored at the laboratory where it's produced."

"I know."

"That gives us a window of opportunity," continues Layla. "If we blow up that lab, we'll stop them in their tracks. It'll take weeks for them to replace it all at a different facility. That should be enough time for us to establish the facts and warn everyone."

"We?" I ask. "So, you're going to help with this?"

"Not exactly. I'm sending Trix to you with a special present. A short-range missile we acquired on the black market. She knows how to use it."

Kieran grins. "Trix is on her way here?"

Layla doesn't reply. She doesn't like to repeat herself. "Zac, there's something else I need to tell you. While you were in Arcadia, we tracked down your mum and brother. They're being held in a quarantine facility in the East Midlands."

Mum. Joe. I haven't seen them for months.

"Are they okay?"

"From what I can tell. But their stay in quarantine is due to end shortly. They'll be transferred to a maximum-security prison. If we want to rescue them, it has to happen now."

I can't quite take it in. "Now?"

"The missile that Layla is bringing to you would be enough to breach the defences of the facility they're at. You could use it there instead of at Bird Laboratories. But we only have the one."

My head feels like it's going to explode. "But if we use the missile there, we have no way to destroy the rest of the vaccine."

"It's a hard decision. That's why you need to be sure that destroying the lab is the right thing to do."

How can she expect me to choose between rescuing my family and saving the world?

Whatever I do feels wrong.

"I-I-I don't know what to say," I admit.

"It'll take Trix the rest of the day to get to you. You have until then to decide. One missile. One target. You get to decide which."

"You're putting me in an impossible position."

"I'm telling you the facts." Layla reaches forward. "I need to end this call. Any longer and we could be traced."

The screen goes blank.

I lean on the table, my head in my hands.

Kieran puts his hand on my back. "That's a tough call, bro."

He knows I'd do anything—*anything*—to save my mum and my brother. Not a day goes by when I don't think of them and what they must be going through. I'd never forgive myself if I passed up the one opportunity I had to free them. But what's the point of rescuing them if everyone is going to die a few weeks later because I didn't stop the vaccine?

My heart is saying one thing, my head another.

"You know whatever you decide, I'll back you one hundred per cent." Kieran is saying all the right things, but he's not helping.

"Well, you shouldn't." I force the words out. "We *have* to destroy the lab. That's more important than anything else." I turn around to face him, grabbing him by the shoulders. "Promise me you won't let me change my mind about this."

"Sure. Ok. I promise. We blow up the lab." Kieran pulls back, a bit surprised by my reaction.

"Given how important that is, I'm surprised Layla even mentioned your family. Surely she knew it would be a distraction."

He's right. Why would she do that?

I wipe my eyes with the sleeve of my hoodie. "I'm being stupid. She doesn't have a clue where my mum and brother are. She's just checking I'm not working for the Collective."

Kieran frowns. "How's that?"

"Don't you see? If I wasn't a hundred per cent sure that the vaccine will kill thousands of people then I'd never target the lab instead of the quarantine centre."

"That's sneaky."

"It's out of order, is what it is. Using my family like that." I sniff and look away. "She doesn't care."

The screen flickers back to life. To my horror, Layla is back.

"I do care, Zac," she says. "But more depends on this than you can know. I had to be sure."

"You heard all that?" asks Kieran.

"Every word."

"So *now* you believe me?"

"I know you believe what you're telling us,"

she allows. "I still don't know that it's true. But you're a bright kid, Zac. I trust your instincts. I think you'd know if you were being played by the Collective."

"What happens now?" asks Kieran.

"Same as before. You wait for Trix. But there's one more thing: I know nothing about this mission. You didn't get any help from me. This call never happened."

"Why?" asks Kieran.

"Cypher will end our branch of the Resistance if he finds out we helped you to destroy the lab. As far as he's concerned, we don't know where you are or what you're up to."

"But you're sending Trix," points out Kieran.

"Trix is a capable Resistance fighter who went AWOL after stealing some of our weapons," argues Layla. "That's the official line."

"So, we're on our own."

Layla picks up on my tone. "Chin up, McAllister. I'm sending you a missile. Complete your mission. Then, we'll smooth things over with Cypher."

Her no-nonsense tone snaps me out of my self-pity. "Yes, ma'am."

"And Kieran, while I'm sure you'll be pleased to see Trix, make sure you stay focused on the task at hand."

He grins. "Yes, ma'am."

"I'm serious. Business before pleasure. Or I'll sell you to Cypher myself."

EIGHTEEN

It's a good day.

I can't remember the last time I spent a day relaxing. I lie on the sofa, enjoying the peace. The patio doors are open, leading out to a large garden. Danny has persuaded Kieran to play football with him. I'm glad someone did; I felt guilty for turning him down, but I didn't have the energy.

Maria wanders in and hands me a cool glass of lemonade. "How are you feeling?"

"Like I'm in heaven."

She laughs. "Some of those cuts and bruises on your chest look nasty. Mind if I look?"

"If you like." I figure she's already seen me naked, and it's been way too long since anyone showed any genuine interest in my welfare. I lift my T-shirt and glance down at my thin, battered body.

"You need to look after yourself," she says. "These could have got infected. How did you even do this?"

"I think I got those jumping on a train," I say, "but it might have been when we climbed a cliff."

She shakes her head, bewildered. "I'm going to use some antiseptic, just to be safe."

"Thanks."

The cream stings as she applies it, but it reminds me of happier days where Mum would treat my cuts.

"You're a brave boy," she says. I'm not sure if she's saying that because I don't flinch with the pain, or because of what we've been through. Either way, it's nice to get a compliment.

"We appreciate this. You rescuing us and everything."

"I wish you could stay longer, but I'm told you have some urgent mission."

I snort. "We always do." Then, curiosity gets the better of me. "Have you been in the Resistance for long?"

"Since the start of the lockdown. Jake's a

delivery driver, so he can transport stuff much more easily than most people. He sometimes sneaks packages for the Resistance."

And kidnaps teenage boys.

I almost say it, but don't. They've been kind to us and I don't want her to think I'm holding a grudge.

"Where is he now?" I ask.

"He's gone to fetch your friend from a pick-up point. He should be back in a couple of hours." She looks me in the eye as she finishes rubbing in the cream. "Layla says you're doing some important work for the Resistance."

"Really?" I'm a little surprised. I'd never realised Layla appreciated what we did.

"It's good that you are. I want the world to be a better place for Danny." Maria puts the lid back on the cream and looks outside, where Kieran is swinging the kid around. "If the lockdown doesn't end soon, he's never going to have a normal life."

"It'll happen. One day." I say it with much more certainty than I feel. It's what I've always told myself. It's the hope that keeps me alive.

"Do you need anything else?" she asks,

standing up.

"Just a week of sleep," I admit.

"Have a doze. There's nothing you can do until your friend arrives."

I rest my head back on the cushion and allow myself to drift off.

***

When I wake, it's getting dark outside.

There are voices coming from the kitchen. I drag myself off the sofa. I still ache, but it's a different ache now, the kind you get when you work out.

The lounge door is ajar, and I pad towards it. As I step into the kitchen, I see Maria, Jake, Kieran and Trix all sat around a table. There's no sign of Danny but I guess he's already in bed.

Trix looks up as I enter. "Look who's back from paradise."

I give her a sheepish smile. "Arcadia wasn't all it was cracked up to be."

"Utopias never are." She pushes back her chair so she can stand up and give me a hug. "It's good to see you."

"And you, Trix."

Kieran raises his eyebrows. "Oi, bro, hands off my girl."

"*Your* girl?" Trix grabs hold of his ear and twists it around, pulling him out of his chair.

Kieran pulls a face. "Sorry, I didn't mean that. Please let me go."

"Only if you admit to being *my* boy."

"Sure. Whatever."

Trix releases him and Kieran rubs his ear.

I take a seat at the table, examining the map that has been spread across it.

"This is Bird Laboratories," says Jake, pointing to a building near the centre. "We were just working out the best place to fire the missile."

"It can't be too far away," adds Trix. "It only has a limited range."

I've got so many questions, I don't know which to ask. "How will we get there?"

"I'll take you in the van," says Jake. "We'll pull over at the side of the road, not too far from the lab, and fire it from there."

I peer at the large rectangle. "It looks like a big place. Will one missile be enough?"

"More than enough," mutters Trix. "It's a serious weapon."

"But won't lots of people die?" I ask.

Kieran shrugs. "We'll fire it in the middle of the night, when most of the workers are at home."

I gulp. "Most?"

Trix slams her fists on the table and glares at me. "Yes, most, Zac. There will still be some security guards. But what can we do? We can hardly give them warning, can we?"

She's not mad at me. She's angry because she doesn't want their blood on her hands, but can't see any way out of it.

"I guess not," I mutter. "I just don't want anyone to die."

"Better a few guards lose their lives than the entire population," points out Kieran. "It's the best we can do, given the situation."

I try to take my mind off it. "What if we get stopped at checkpoints on the way to the launch site?"

Jake answers that one. "Apparently you're a pretty accomplished hacker. We need you to forge a delivery authorisation for the crates in my van. Then everything should check out on the system."

"That'll take hours," I groan.

Kieran slaps me on the back. "Best get started, then, hadn't you?"

"They're big crates," says Jake. "We'll pretend I'm shipping heavy lab equipment to Bird Laboratories. That should give us a great excuse to get close."

"What's really in the crates?" I ask.

"One of them contains the missile and the launch apparatus," says Trix.

"What about the others? What's in them?"

Jake looks up at me and smiles. "You and your friends."

NINETEEN

It's past midnight when we clamber into the back of the van. A couple of LED strips line the van's hold, giving off a harsh unnatural glow. Stacked along the sides are several wooden crates.

Jake pulls out a crowbar, and pops the lid off one. Inside, there's a single cushion. "In you get."

I gulp. "Seriously?"

"Afraid so. You never know when an over-enthusiastic guard will want to check the van at a checkpoint, even with our fake paperwork."

"It's only for a few hours," points out Kieran. "Besides, I don't know what you're moaning about. You're a skinny runt. Imagine what it'll be like for me and Trix."

I grin at him. "Why? You getting in a crate together?"

He smiles back. "Now that's not a bad idea." He turns to Trix. "What do you think?"

Trix raises her eyebrows. "I think I'd kill you."

"Separate crates it is, then."

I climb into the crate, then hunker down on the cushion. Jake replaces the lid and nails it down.

"Hey," I object. "Do you have to do that?"

"Makes it less likely the guards will try to open it," he replies. "I'm also going to stack another box on top."

I don't like the idea of being trapped in this prison, but it could be worse, I guess. I can't stretch out, but there is some space to move. Thin gaps between the wooden slats provide plenty of ventilation.

Still, there's nothing to do and no hope of going back to sleep. For the next couple of hours, I'll just have to sit here. I wonder if I'll be able to chat to the others, but as the van starts to move the noise of the engine makes it impossible to hear anything else. And every time the vehicle turns a corner, I'm thrown from side to side. So much for taking better care of myself.

I jam my legs into one corner of the crate and

my body in the other to minimise the movement. Then, I wait it out, hoping we'll make it to Bird Laboratories without being caught.

***

When the van stops, I wonder if we're there.

But it doesn't feel like we've been in the van for more than an hour.

As the engine turns off, I listen carefully. There's the murmuring of human voices, then footsteps.

Someone climbs into the back of the van.

"You could have anything in these crates." That's not Jake's voice. It's someone else. "I'll need to check them out."

"It's just lab equipment," replies Jake. "You've got all the details on your system. I'd appreciate it if you just let us through. We're running late as it is."

"I'm not sure." A bright light filters between the slats. Someone is shining a flashlight at my crate. I wonder if he's trying to peer in.

I don't move. The slightest sound could give me away.

This is bad. If the guard opens any of the crates, then it's game over. I can hear him scrabbling around, trying to lift the lid off.

"You got a crowbar to open this?" asks the officer.

"Nope," replies Jake. "Don't need one. I just transport them."

For a moment, I think we've gotten away with it. If the man can't open the crates, then we're safe.

"I've got one in my cabin. Wait here."

A few seconds later, I hear Jake hissing to us. "Don't move, don't speak, and don't do anything stupid. I've got this."

I want to remind him I couldn't do anything even if I wanted to because I'm nailed in a box, but I've been told to keep quiet. Even Kieran keeps his mouth shut.

Time stands still.

We're all locked in our own misery, waiting for the man to return.

Eventually, he does.

"Right, let's look inside this one." To my horror, I feel the man tap the side of my crate.

"Sure. No problem. Let me just take the other

one off it." A bit of puffing and panting later, the crate above me has been moved aside.

Now, there's the sound of metal being forced under the lid. Light spills into my hiding place as the corner is pulled up, creating a small gap. Then the crowbar moves further along and is levered again, popping the lid even higher. Now, the guard leans forward, shining a light in my face.

"What the..." he exclaims, as he realises he's looking at a boy.

As I squint at his pudgy face, I see the expression change again; from shock to confusion to anger. Then, he staggers backwards, away from the crate. As he turns around, I see a needle sticking out his back.

"You... you..." The man can't get the sentence out. Instead, he collapses. Jake catches him and lowers him to the floor.

"What happened?" I ask, still blinking as my eyes adjust to the bright flashlight.

"I gave him a shot of tranquilliser. He'll be out for a few hours. Can you climb out and give me a hand?"

"Sure." I squeeze my way out of the opening,

relieved to stretch my limbs.

"Grab his legs," says Jake. "We need to dump him back in his cabin."

"Won't the other guards see us?"

"Luckily for us, there aren't any. This is only a small checkpoint. Come on, let's move."

The guard is overweight, and we have to drag him in short bursts out of the van and back into the small cabin next to the road. Once he's inside, we drop him on the floor.

Jake points at the controls. "As soon as I'm back in the van, raise the barrier, so I can drive through. Once we're on the other side, we'll get you back in your crate."

"Sure." I watch as he jogs back to the driver's door and climbs in. He starts the engine and gives me the thumbs up.

The controls are simple enough. I hit the green button, and the barrier lifts, allowing him to drive through. As soon as he's through, I lower it again. Then I dash out of the cabin and duck under the barrier myself.

Jake opens the back of the van and I clamber in.

"Won't someone figure out something's

wrong?" I ask.

"For sure. Guards have to check in every half hour. When this guy doesn't respond, they'll send someone to look. We've just got to hope we're far enough away by then."

"Do I really need to get back in the crate?"

"Afraid so. There may be more checkpoints."

I ease myself back under the lid, tearing my T-shirt on a nail. I knew these nice clothes wouldn't last long. The crate feels even more cramped than before as Jake secures the lid.

Suck it up, Zac.

I might be uncomfortable, but we got through the checkpoint.

The mission is on track.

And that's all that matters.

TWENTY

It's another hour before we reach our destination.

All the time, I'm being thrown around in the tiny space, and I've got at least three splinters in my hands from the rough wood.

I hear Jake levering the lids off the other crates first, letting out Kieran and Trix.

When he opens my crate, my legs are numb with cramp and I struggle to clamber over the side of the box. I stagger towards the open doors in the darkness, the only light coming from the dim LED strips.

Trix and Kieran are waiting outside, and they help me out.

"Pleasant journey?" asks Kieran, with a grin.

I punch him on the shoulder. "Better than on

the back of your bike."

That makes Trix laugh. "He's right about that."

I look around. We're on a quiet country lane near the top of a small hill. There's a thin crescent moon giving off just enough light to see. Fields stretch out on either side, reminding me of the times Kieran and I spent running the routes for the Resistance.

Further down the hill, I can see a brightly lit industrial complex. It's huge, the size of a power station.

"Bird Laboratories, I'm guessing," I mutter.

Kieran gives me a push. "You see, Trix? I told you Zac was a genius."

"Hmm." Trix isn't listening. She's holding up binoculars, checking out the target. It's impossible to tell what she's thinking.

"Does everything look okay?" I ask.

She ignores the question. "Let's get the missile set up."

We climb back into the van, where Jake is levering the lid off another crate. Inside is a stack of metal poles.

"What are those for?" I ask, wondering if he's

147

opened the wrong box.

"The launch tower. We have to build it before we can fire the missile."

My heart sinks. "I thought it would be a handheld launcher."

Trix pulls out some of the metal tubes. "This is a serious weapon; much too big for that. If we get this right, it will raze that entire complex to the ground. There's no room for error; it needs a stable launchpad. Help me get these outside."

I do as I'm told. Between me and Kieran, we move them to a huge pile at the roadside. Then the fun really starts as Trix orders us around, telling us which bit goes where. It's like putting up a tent in the dark.

When we finish, we've built something that looks like the skeleton of a pyramid. It reaches almost as high as the van.

"I always wanted to see the Eiffel tower," jokes Kieran.

"Will you be serious, just for once," snaps Trix.

Kieran glances at me. He's wondering why she's in such a bad mood. I think I already know.

"Are there many people down there?" I ask as we clamber inside the van to fetch the missile.

Trix looks away. "You don't want to know."

She's right. I don't. Not really. Thinking about it makes me feel guilty.

I feel even worse when I see the size of the missile. It's in a crate almost the entire length of the van. It's protected by insulated foam, cut perfectly to size.

"We have to lift this carefully," says Jake.

"No kidding," says Kieran. "If we drop it, I'm guessing we all die?"

Neither Trix nor Jake answer, which confirms his suspicions.

We take our positions, ready to pick it up.

"On three," says Jake. "Bring it up slow and steady. One... two... three..."

We take hold of the cold metal and lift. It's heavier than I expect. Even with all four of us, we're only just able to carry it.

As Jake and Kieran step out of the van, we miscalculate and I hear the bottom of the missile scrape against the floor.

Jake swears. "Lift it higher!"

We do, but my arms ache like crazy. I don't know how long I can keep this up.

Somehow, we get it outside. We lay it on the

ground for a few minutes while our arms recover. Then, we go again, this time lifting the missile upright and attaching it to the clips on the launch tower.

Trix pulls out a laptop, crouches on the floor and opens it up. I watch over her shoulder.

"You access the missile controls through this," she says, clicking on an app. "First, I have to calibrate the missile, then lock it on to the target. After that, we're ready to launch. These controls here set the countdown." She points to the screen.

"How long will all the prep take?" I ask.

"I don't know," she admits. "I've never done this. Howard showed me the basics, but we only had the one missile, so we couldn't practice."

I stand up and use the binoculars to scope out Bird Laboratories. I can't see any movement, but there's a guard sitting in the security booth watching TV. He has no idea what's about to happen.

I let out a sigh. "That poor guy. He's going to die, isn't he?"

"He's not the only one. There must be a few security guards on a site that size."

"Maybe we could save them?" I suggest.

Trix is dismissive, as usual. "Sure. I'll send him an email telling him we're about to blow the place up."

"I didn't mean that. I just wondered if we could get them as far away from the explosion as possible. Is there any part of the site that won't be destroyed?"

"Hard to say for sure. But it's a long, thin campus. A person might stand some chance at the furthest corner." She points to it on the map.

I study it. "I'm going to go down there and create a diversion. With any luck, they'll come and investigate."

"What kind of diversion?" asks Kieran.

"I'll mess with the fence or something. Set off the alarm."

Trix pulls a face. "Even if you do, they won't send *all* the security team."

I shrug. "If I save one person, it'll be worth it."

"As soon as the missile is ready, I'm going to launch it. So, you'd better be quick."

"I'm on it." I turn to Jake. "You got any bolt cutters?"

"I think I might." He jumps back into the van

and rummages around behind the seat. He pulls some out and hands them over. "You're not going to get yourself killed, are you, Zac?"

"Nope." I grin. "Just badly maimed."

He rolls his eyes. "Don't even joke about that."

I glance over at Kieran. "You coming?"

He hesitates, unsure whether Trix wants him to stay.

"Don't hang around here on my account," she tells him. "You'll just get in my way."

"In that case, I'll look after Zac. Someone needs to keep that boy in line."

I sigh with relief.

Kieran might be annoying, but he's the best friend I've got.

And I don't want to head into the darkness alone.

TWENTY-ONE

It's further than it looks to the fence.

The complex is also much bigger than I thought. As we run towards the enormous buildings, I feel small and vulnerable. The missile might be powerful, but is it going to be able to destroy the entire place?

Kieran tugs on my hoodie, pulling me aside. "I think we need to come away from the road. If we get any closer, they might see us."

I know he's right, but I also know that progress will be a lot slower if we cut across the fields. "If we follow the fence round to the left, it dips a little further down the hill. That corner will be furthest from the explosion."

We jog across the dirt, trying not to turn our ankles on the uneven ground. At the other side of the field, a bramble hedge blocks our way. We have to find a way through. That's not easy, especially without using a flashlight.

"I think the branches are sparser here," mutters Kieran, from further along. "We can slide under."

It's not as easy as it sounds. Thorns cling to my clothes and scratch at my hands and face as I commando crawl through the undergrowth. By the time I pull myself out the other side, I feel like a pin cushion. Kieran doesn't look any better; his face has some nasty scratches and a line of blood drips from his forehead.

"This security guard better be grateful," he mutters.

"At least there are no other hedges," I point out. "It's straightforward from here."

Kieran says something else under his breath, cursing me for coming up with this crazy idea, but I ignore him and press on. The chain-link fence is at least four metres high, with coils of lethal-looking barbed wire perched on top. There's no way over, but I don't plan to climb it. I grasp the bolt cutters as I walk towards the furthest corner of the site. Once I'm in the right place, I crouch down and snip. One by one, the metal wires break. I'm creating a hole that would be big enough to get through, even though I have no intention of going inside.

Kieran stands behind me, looking nervous. "I'm not hearing any sirens," he says.

"I'm hoping I've set off a silent alarm. There's no way they have this level of security and nothing to stop people cutting their way through the fence."

"If you say so." He doesn't sound so sure.

But seconds later, we both discover what stops people from breaking in. There's a strange noise. At first, I think it's drops of water landing on the ground, like it's started raining. But it's not that. It's feet. Paws, in fact.

There's a snarl and a growl as a dog leaps at the fence, making the entire section shake. Then it barks. Loud enough for the whole county to hear. I stop cutting. I'm already wondering if I've made too much of a hole and whether the dog will get out.

Kieran is thinking the same thing. "Run!"

We hear shouts in the distance and see flashlights bobbing up and down as security guards follow hot on the dog's heels.

I run, stumbling through the field and scrambling back under the bramble hedge. This time I don't even feel the thorns clawing at my flesh. I get through at record speed, Kieran close behind. There's no sign of the dog. I don't think it got through the hole. A few more cuts and it would have been a different story.

"Got any more great ways to get us killed?" asks Kieran, gasping for breath as we reach the road.

"Let's hope they're close enough to that corner to stay alive," I say.

We jog towards the van.

I'm expecting the missile to soar over our heads at any moment.

But, it doesn't.

That's bad news. If Trix isn't ready and we've put the lab on high alert, we might have endangered the plan. I pick up my pace, desperate to get back.

Without warning, Kieran grabs hold of me and pulls me aside.

"What now?" I hiss. "We need to tell Trix to fire the missile."

"Don't you think she already knows? She told us she wasn't going to wait. Something's wrong."

I can hear voices in the distance; snatches of conversation on the breeze.

"That doesn't sound like Trix or Jake," I whisper to Kieran.

We creep up the road, silent as shadows. I can make out the silhouette of the van, and the strange shape of the launch tower next to it. Now, the conversation is clearer.

"You know what I'm asking." Even though it's not one of our friends, the voice is familiar. I've heard it somewhere before. "How do we disable the launch sequence?"

"You can't. Once it's set, there's no way to stop it." Trix has barely finished speaking before she cries out in pain.

Kieran makes a move as if he's going to rush to her aid, but I grab his arm and pull him back. I lock eyes with him.

Don't mess this up.

He grits his teeth, but reins in his anger. For now.

"Every time you lie to me, my men will cause you increasing amounts of pain. Do you understand?" The voice is cold, more robot than human.

"Cypher." I mouth the word to Kieran.

He nods.

Trix is trying to reason with the Resistance leader. "Unless we fire this missile and destroy the last of the poisoned vaccine, everyone will die. You. Me. All your men. Everyone you love."

"You've spent too long with your little friend, Zachary McAllister. In a minute, you'll tell me where he is. But first, you're going to disable the missile."

Another cry of pain. Kieran gnaws on his fist.

"STOP! I'll tell you," sobs Trix. "There's a set of three buttons on the side. Hold in the first and third button for five seconds, then press the middle one when it flashes."

"Do as she says," Cypher orders one of his men. Then, he turns back to Trix. "If you're lying, I'm going to break your arm."

It's then that I see something glinting in the moonlight, half-buried in the hedge. I point it out to Kieran, then scurry over to pick it up. It's the laptop. Trix must have thrown it away the moment she sensed danger.

I flip it open, careful to keep the van between me and Cypher's men. The preliminary checks are complete, and the target has been set but the launch sequence hasn't been initiated.

I have to finish the job. I set the timer to twenty seconds, then click 'LAUNCH'.

"The missile is going to go off any second," I whisper to Kieran. "While they're distracted, get in the van and see if the keys are there. If they are, use it to create as much chaos as you can."

He nods, glad to have something he can do to save Trix.

I sneak a look around the side of the van. Cypher's lackey is shining a flashlight on the sleek black casing of the missile. "I can't see any buttons."

"They're on the other side," says Trix, her voice wavering. She knows they're about to discover she's bluffing.

I check the laptop.

Five... Four...

"Still no buttons."

Three... Two...

"Break her arm."

One...

Someone screams.

TWENTY-TWO

It's not Trix.

It's the man who was standing next to the missile.

The rocket shoots into the air with a trail of white-hot flame and a cloud of dust.

The man shrieks as he emerges from the launch tower, his clothes on fire. He rolls on the floor, trying to put out the flames. Meanwhile, the missile soars through the air, heading straight for Bird Laboratories.

"No!" Cypher is furious. He lifts a gun and shoots, hoping to knock it out of the air. But no one could hit it from this distance. He turns on Trix, who is still being held by one of his men. "Do you know what you've done?"

Trix is gloriously defiant. "We've saved the

world."

"You stupid girl. You've ruined everything. And now, you'll pay."

Whatever he has in mind will have to wait because the missile hits its target. I see it before I hear it: a white circle almost as bright as the sun, right at the heart of the complex. It grows bigger, a halo of light emanating from the centre.

I drop to the ground, roll under the van and slam my hands over my ears. Even with them covered, I feel like my eardrums will burst. The ground shakes beneath me and the roar gets so loud that I wonder if the explosion will engulf us as well as the laboratories. Maybe we didn't park far enough away? I can feel hot air and dust being blown into my hiding place, making it hard to breathe.

It can't last much longer.

When the noise dies away, I hear something else: the engine. Kieran is about to drive the van forward and I'm stuck underneath. If I try to roll out, he might run me over. I stay on the ground, as low as I can, hoping the exhaust won't hit me.

The wheels spin and the van shoots forward. There's a thud and then it stops. There's more shouting.

I jump to my feet and creep to the front of the vehicle. I peer out from the passenger side.

The man who was holding Trix is on the ground, holding his leg. It looks like he took the full force of the impact. Trix is free from his grip, but is frozen in place, her back to the van. Cypher is only a few metres away, pointing a gun at her.

"One more step and I'm going to shoot," he warns. "Tell your friend to get out of the van and join us."

"You'd better do as he says," says Trix, her voice shaking.

I hear the driver's door open as Kieran climbs down.

"Cool it, Cypher," soothes Kieran. "We're on the same side. We all work for the Resistance."

"And if we don't get moving, all of us will be caught," urges Trix.

Cypher pauses, weighing up his options. "You disobeyed direct orders. You aided a traitor and a runaway. You deserve to be court-martialled and shot."

"Maybe," says Trix, "but not here."

While they're talking, I sneak behind the van,

then slip across the road into the trees. I creep forwards, staying low, circling behind the crazed Resistance leader. There's not as much undergrowth as I'd like and it's not easy staying hidden, but there's a lot of smoke and noise. The man who got burnt is still crying out in pain on the other side of the road.

"It's over, Cypher," shouts Kieran. "The lab is destroyed. You lost this battle. It's time to lick your wounds and go home."

"First, I have to clean up." Cypher straightens his arm; he's about to shoot.

I jump on his back, knocking his hand sideways. The gun fires, smashing a headlight. I cling to his back, but Cypher is twice my size. Within seconds, he's getting control of the situation, dropping to the floor to shake me off. Fortunately, Trix and Kieran race to my aid. Trix relieves him of the gun and points it at his head.

"I should put you out of your misery," she says. "Just like you were going to do to me."

Cypher laughs, a harsh metallic sound. His robot eye gleams in the darkness. "You think I'm afraid of you? You can't kill me, little girl."

"Are you sure about that?" Trix doesn't

hesitate. She shoots Cypher, not once but three times. His body gyrates, then lies still, blood pooling underneath him. She kicks him with her foot. "Seems you were wrong."

"Trix..." Kieran steps back, horrified. "You just killed the leader of the Resistance."

"I killed a psycho." Trix looks around, checking whether any of Cypher's men are a threat. One is dying from burns. The other has been knocked down and is squirming on the floor in agony.

"What happened to Jake?" I ask. I realise I haven't seen him since Kieran and I returned.

"He's in the van," says Trix. "They knocked him out, but I think he's alive."

I think of five-year-old Danny and breathe a sigh of relief. "So, what now?"

"We get the hell out of here."

TWENTY-THREE

The van squeals as we take the corner way too fast. I clutch the laptop to stop it from falling off my lap.

"Can you even drive?" asks Kieran.

"Can you shut up?" Trix is gripping the steering wheel, her eyes focused on the road. "Have you logged in yet, Zac?"

"Give me a chance!" It's almost impossible to type with the van veering all over the road. "If you drive slower, it might help."

"You realise I have no idea where I'm heading?" demands Trix, through gritted teeth. "So, can you stop with the excuses and ask Layla for a destination?"

She's more stressed than I've ever seen her. If I answer back, she might punch me in the face, and that could cause us to crash. It's not worth the risk. "Sure."

I tap away on the keyboard, accessing the secure site that puts me in touch with our branch of the Resistance.

"Well?" demands Trix.

"I've posted the message and our co-ordinates. Now, we have to wait for a reply."

"Did you encrypt it?"

"No. I thought I'd let everyone else read it. And I also emailed the Collective, so they'd know where they could find us."

Trix takes her eyes off the road just long enough to scare me. "Can the sarcasm or you'll be walking."

Kieran is sitting between us. "Come on, everyone. Let's stay friends."

Trix doesn't like that either. "I told *you* to shut up."

He glances at me and shrugs. There's no reasoning with Trix when she's like this. Something on the screen catches my attention. "They've sent us a location: a metro station. We need to head to the underground platform."

"That doesn't make sense," says Trix. "No

passenger trains run during lockdown. And they don't run freight through the underground."

"Maybe there's another Resistance base down there?" suggests Kieran.

"You need to take a right up ahead," I tell her. "Then, follow the road for a couple of miles."

A loud groan from behind startles me. I'd forgotten that Jake was back there.

"Are you okay?" I call back to him.

"I've been better." He sits up. "What's happening?"

"We got away," I explain. "Layla has sent us co-ordinates for a rendezvous. We're going to get rescued."

"If we live that long," quips Kieran.

"Any more comments like that and you won't," says Trix.

Jake must have taken a serious blow; I can see him rubbing his head in the darkness. "I have a killer headache. I don't feel so good."

"For what it's worth, neither do I," mutters Kieran. "I don't like the sound of the underground."

"Me neither," I admit. "But what other option do we have? Layla's never let us down in the past.

She must have a reason for sending us there."

"What do we do when we get there?" asks Trix, always two steps ahead.

I re-read the message and gulp. "You don't want to know."

***

Trix careers into the kerb, almost jolting me off the seat.

We're surrounded by tall, dark buildings; the remnants of a high street. No one lives here, and these shops haven't been open for years. The windows are boarded up or protected by metal shutters.

As we climb out the van, I glance around. If anyone is squatting in these buildings, they'll have heard the van for sure. But squatters don't call the police or the Quarantine Agency. They just mug you for food.

We walk towards the underground station.

Jake hesitates. "I'm going to leave you guys to it. This part doesn't involve me and I need to get back to my family."

"Won't they come after you?" I ask.

"Maybe. But I'm just a delivery driver. And without you in the van, I have nothing to hide."

Trix nods. "We appreciate your help."

"You've been amazing," I add. "Thank you so much." I step forward and pull him into a hug. I wish I could go back with him and be a part of his family, but that's never going to happen.

"You kids take care of yourselves." Jake climbs into the driver's seat. "Maybe one day we'll meet again."

"I hope so," I tell him.

Seconds later, he drives away.

"How do we access the station?" asks Kieran.

I check Layla's message. "There's a false panel on a window. Around the back. The third window from the fire escape, apparently."

We head down a narrow alleyway.

"The third window?" checks Trix.

"Yep."

"This one." She tries to tug out the wooden board that covers it, but it won't budge. "You sure this is right?"

Kieran gives her a hand, but even together they can't pull the panel away.

Why can't anything be easy?

"Let me see that message," demands Trix, grabbing the laptop from my hands and opening it. While she crouches on the floor, studying the screen, I check out the boarded window for myself. There's no point just tugging on it. If Trix and Kieran can't shift it, there's no way I will. But maybe there's some kind of mechanism?

It turns out it's even simpler than that. The board is slotted in grooves at the top and bottom. When I lift it, the bottom comes free, and I can slide it out. The window behind has been left open so we don't even need to break any glass.

Kieran puts his hand on Trix's shoulder. "Zac's sorted it."

"It wasn't hard," I point out.

Trix slams shut the laptop. "Are you saying we're dumb?"

"I just meant..."

"Who votes Zac goes in first as a reward?" says Kieran, cheerily. He puts up his hand and Trix follows suit.

I squint through the dirty window, but all I can see is blackness. "Do I have to?"

"Someone does. Might as well be you. You are the cleverest, after all."

TWENTY-FOUR

I pull the window wide open and stick my head through the gap. It was eerie in the alleyway. This is downright creepy. I switch on a flashlight and sweep it over dusty chairs and a deserted ticket office.

"See any ghosts?" asks Kieran.

"Not yet."

"Then move your butt."

I clamber in, Trix and Kieran close behind. We jump some turnstiles and make our way down a steep staircase. As we get further underground, the darkness becomes more intense.

A shiver runs down my spine. "I don't like this."

Kieran acts like he's not scared. "It's like when we first went to the pub. That was pretty scary.

But I bet there's a lovely bunch of people squirrelled away in these tunnels."

If there is, there's no sign of them when we reach the platform. Worse still, this place doesn't look like anyone has been here for years. I shine my flashlight from one end to the other, hoping for some sign of the Resistance.

"What now?" asks Kieran.

I don't want to answer that question, but Trix answers for me. She's read all the messages herself.

"We have to jump down on to the tracks and walk along the tunnel."

"Isn't that just peachy?" mutters Kieran. He shines a light on to the rails and something scurries away.

"Rats," says Trix. "I bet there are loads of them down here."

"Yeah, and I bet they're hungry."

"They won't attack us if we're moving," insists Trix. "We're much bigger than they are." She jumps down from the platform, landing between the rails. "Follow me."

I lower myself carefully off the edge.

Kieran laughs at me as he drops on to the

tracks. "Want a cushion to break your fall?"

"Shut it," I say. "I'm much smaller than you."

"And much lighter," he points out. "That should make it easier."

I ignore him, dropping the rest of the way and pushing past to follow Trix into the tunnel.

Our flashlights only reach so far. Either side of the tracks are curved brick walls. I'm glad that no trains come down here during lockdown, because there's no way to escape. We'd be dead for sure.

There are way too many rats, and they seem to get braver by the minute. Trix kicks out with her foot, knocking one away.

"Are you sure the rats won't attack?" asks Kieran, sounding nervous.

"We'll be fine," insists Trix, but I notice she picks up her pace.

The tunnel is endless. The further we walk, the more hopeless we feel. There's no sign of the Resistance. I can't help wondering if we'll die down here, our carcasses being torn to pieces by the hungry rodents.

Then, I hear it.

So do the others.

The loud roar of an approaching train.

"That's impossible," says Kieran. "It can't be."

Trix swears. "We have to get off the tracks. Now!"

I sweep my flashlight around the narrow tunnel. "There's nowhere to go!"

The noise is getting louder, echoing off the walls. I see headlights in the distance. We don't have long.

"Run!" shouts Trix.

I don't need telling twice. I turn and bolt up the tunnel. Kieran and Trix are right behind.

But we've come a long way, and no one can outrun a train. When I glance over my shoulder, I see it bearing down on us. It's too close now; it'll never stop in time. We're about to get squashed, or smashed into a million pieces.

Our lives are over.

In my desperation, I lose my footing and land on the rails. There's no point getting back up. It's already too late.

I close my eyes and prepare to die.

TWENTY-FIVE

It stops.

That doesn't make sense: a train can't just screech to a halt.

I roll over, shielding my eyes from the bright headlights.

The engine cuts out, and I can hear my own desperate gasps for breath.

"Zac, boy, what yer doin' lying down there?"

It's a voice I'd recognise anywhere. "Del?"

I can see his silhouette as he walks towards us. Gradually, I piece together what's happened. It wasn't a train that was coming down the tunnel; it was a group of motorbikes. That explains how they stopped so fast. Del, Bernie and Leo, our friends from the Resistance, have come to find us.

"Are you guys alright?" asks Leo.

"I think I need some clean underwear," says Kieran, "but otherwise I'm fine."

That makes the bikers laugh.

"Layla sent us to get ya," explains Del. "We 'ave to take yer back to the pub."

"Sounds good to me," I say, climbing to my feet and dusting myself off. "But what about the roadblocks?"

"Don't yer worry about them," says Del, slapping me on the back so hard it almost knocks me over. "We won't be takin' no roads. We ride along the tracks."

He hauls me onto the back of his bike by the seat of my jeans. I wish he wouldn't do that. I hate being hauled around like a rag doll. But right now, I'm just glad to be with friends, and to have an escape plan.

Once everyone is ready, they kick the engines into life and we shoot down the tunnel. I can't see anything around Del's massive body, but I don't want to. I'm happy just to hold on and let him carry me to safety.

***

It's a long journey.

Only the cool night air and the threat of falling from the saddle keeps me awake.

The noise from the engines makes it impossible to talk, but in some ways that's a relief. I have nothing to say. I just want to be back at the pub with Layla and my Resistance buddies.

When we leave the tracks, we're close to my hometown. From here, it's only a short ride to Bayliss Road, the location of the secret base. The motorbikes pull behind some abandoned shops and draw to a halt by a row of garages.

As soon as the vehicles are stowed away, we slip down the dark street to the derelict pub. From outside, it looks like no one has been inside for years. That's all part of the illusion. The windows are boarded up and graffiti is sprawled across the walls. To gain access, we sneak around the back and open a hatch to an old beer cellar. Even this looks dark and dingy; the kind of place you'd never want to go. The first time Kieran and I came to this place, we were freaked out.

As we walk through a heavy black door into a basement corridor, bars descend from the roof, blocking the way ahead, caging us in. We have to wait for the Resistance security guys to come and check us out before we can go any further. Del and the others are allowed in straight away, but Kieran, Trix and I get the full treatment, sensor batons waved over our bodies checking for hidden devices.

"It's good to see you again, Zac," says Gavin, the soldier who's checking me.

"It's good to be back."

"Hey, Gavin," says Kieran, with a cheeky smile, "you might want to do a full strip search. I think I saw Zac sticking something up his butt earlier."

Fortunately, Gavin knows he's joking, and I don't have to take off anything other than my shoes.

As soon as the soldiers are satisfied we're not being tracked, we're allowed up the staircase to the large room above. The smell hits me first. It's not great, a mixture of food, sweat and alcohol, but it makes me feel at home. At one end is the bar where they used to serve drinks, complete with dusty glasses and mostly empty bottles lining the shelves behind. Del and his biker buddies have already found their way to their stools and cracked open some beers.

The rest of the space is full of tables and chairs, padded booths and fruit machines. There's even a pool table. It would look like a normal pub if it wasn't for the number of computers spread around. Keyboards, monitors and boxes with flashing lights are on almost every table, power leads trailing across the floor. Even though it's late, a few hackers are still hard at work, transfixed by the code.

It's always dark in here. The windows have been blocked and the place is always gloomy, even during the day. Most of the light comes from computer screens.

"Home, sweet home," says Kieran, wandering towards the booth in the corner where we hang out.

"Not so fast."

I see Layla walking towards us. If she's glad to see us, she doesn't show it. "We need to debrief. Now."

"Can't it wait until the morning?" whines Kieran. "It's been a long night."

Layla steps towards him, her face like thunder. Her bald head glistens with sweat. I've never seen her so worked up. "You shot Cypher, a key leader of the Resistance. So, no, it can't wait."

There's no point arguing. Me, Trix and Kieran follow Layla to a quiet corner where she makes us sit down at an empty table.

"Well?" she demands. "Want to explain yourselves?"

"I already told you about the vaccine," I point out. "You knew we were going to destroy Bird Laboratories. Jake drove us there. While Trix was setting up the missile, Kieran and I tried to create a diversion for some guards, so they didn't get killed."

"An unnecessary risk," says Layla.

"Maybe, but it worked. By the time we got back to the van, we found Cypher and his men had taken Trix and Jake hostage."

"They appeared out of nowhere," cuts in Trix. "I was busy calibrating the missile, ready for launch. The next thing I knew, I heard Jake shout a warning, so I threw the laptop aside before anyone saw it. Seconds later, I had a gun pointing right at me."

"There was no reasoning with Cypher," sighs Kieran. "He was determined to stop us. He was going to make Trix disarm the missile."

"But we had to destroy the vaccine," I cut in. "If that got released, millions of people would die. So, I launched the missile and between us we got control of the situation."

"It was me that shot Cypher," admits Trix. "I killed him."

"He's not dead," says Layla, "but he's not happy."

"Wait, what?" Kieran says what we're all thinking. "That man was a corpse. Trix shot him at point blank range. There's no way he survived that."

Layla shakes her head. "Cypher is alive and well. And he wants your heads on a plate. You realise what you've done? You've started a war."

"*He* started it," insists Kieran.

He's right, but he sounds like a five-year-old on a playground.

"It makes no difference," says Layla. "He's given me an ultimatum. Either I send you three back to him or he'll consider us all traitors."

I've known Layla for a long time, but she doesn't like to let her emotions cloud her judgement. We may not be as safe as I'd hoped.

"What will you do?" asks Trix.

Layla leans back and sighs. "I don't know yet. I need time to think."

Kieran stares at her in amazement. "You're considering it? You'd sell us out just to keep peace with Cypher?"

"If the Resistance crumbles, the Collective will win. It may be a price worth paying." Layla stands up, the interrogation over. "Get some sleep. Whatever happens in the morning, you'll need it."

TWENTY-SIX

Before I go to bed, I need the bathroom.

The pub toilets are as disgusting as ever. No one ever cleans in here, and the bikers aren't exactly careful with their aim. I wrinkle my nose as I step up to the urinal.

I've just about finished my business when I hear the door open behind me. I glance around to see who it is.

Jamie.

The boy is only twelve, a year younger than me. He was kidnapped by the Resistance so I could go to Arcadia in his place.

I always thought he had a rough deal, especially when he was chained here in the toilets until I convinced Layla to let him out. Even then, she wouldn't let him go anywhere unless he was attached to one of us.

Annoyingly, she was right. When I was in Arcadia, I discovered Jamie was a Collective spy, sent to discover the location of our base. He'd been crafty enough to get himself caught deliberately, so he'd be brought here. In the madness of the last few days, that's kind of slipped my mind.

"Hey, Zac," he says. He's still wearing the ripped army clothing I gave him before I left.

I zip up my jeans and head over to wash my hands. "Hey."

"What was Arcadia like?" he asks, all innocent.

"You already know," I say, looking at him in the mirror. "I found out who you really are. You were sent here to hack into our systems and send our location to the Collective."

Jamie gulps. "Have you told anyone?"

"Not yet." I splash water on my face. "But I will. Right now, in fact."

As I step towards the door, he blocks my way.

"Don't do that. Please, Zac. They'll chain me up again."

"If Del doesn't beat you to death first," I point out. "Either way, you deserve it."

He grabs hold of me. "Let me explain."

"Let go, Jamie." As I try to push past, his grip gets tighter. He may be younger than me, but he's just as strong. He slams me against the wall.

"You have to listen."

"So you can tell me more of your lies?" I push back, but Jamie swings me around and gets me in an armlock. He forces me to the floor and kneels on my back, my face inches away from a puddle of something grim.

"I don't want to fight you," he pleads. "And I won't send the Collective any more information. I just don't want to spend the next few months chained in these toilets."

"You should have thought of that before you betrayed us."

He forces my arm higher, making me cry out in pain. "You're such a hypocrite," he says. "You did the same thing to the Collective. You went in there, pretending to be someone else. Did it feel good betraying all the people who were so nice to you?"

"No," I gasp. "I felt guilty the whole time. But I had to do it for my mission."

"You see? We're the same, Zac. You worked for

the Resistance. I worked for the Collective. We both did what he had to, and we both lied to people who trusted us."

I hadn't thought about it like that, but he's right. We've both done our fair share of sneaking around and spying on people.

I wriggle on the floor, trying to get free. It's no use. He has me pinned. "So, what are you planning to do now? Sit on me forever?"

"I just wanted you to hear me out."

To my surprise, he lets go of my arm and stands to his feet. He steps back and leans against the sink. "For what it's worth," he says, "I enjoyed spending time with you and Kieran and Trix. I wasn't faking that." A tear runs down his cheek and I wonder if I'm being played. But it seems genuine. He's just a kid in a difficult situation.

I know how that feels.

If I tell Layla that Jamie is a spy then his life is over. They won't kill him; at least, I don't think they will. But they'll lock him up for sure. They'll interrogate him. And they'll be mad that he lied to them. He won't be freed until the lockdown is over and all of this madness has come to an end.

Who knows how long that will take?

"How did you get Layla to stop chaining you to someone else?" I ask, wondering how he got an opportunity to hack the Resistance system in the first place.

"I offered to help Del in the kitchens. I couldn't do that when I was joined at the ankle." He can see I'm thinking it through, and he drops to his knees. "Please, Zac, I'm begging you. Don't rat me out. I'll do anything for you. Anything."

I can't stand to see him in so much distress. "I won't say anything," I tell him.

Jamie jumps up and gives me a hug. "You're a good friend, Zac. I'm only sorry that we found ourselves on different sides."

I pull away and look him dead in the eye. "There's something you need to know. Things have changed in Arcadia. The founder, Aaron Greaves, has been arrested."

"No way!"

"Eugene has taken over. And he's planning to poison the rest of the population with a fake vaccine."

Jamie's face goes pale. "The Collective are trying to save humanity. They'd never do that."

"*Aaron* would never do that," I correct him. "Neither would a lot of people who live there. We both know that. But Eugene is different. He's convinced it's the only way to save the planet. And now he's in charge, I don't think anyone can stop him except the Resistance."

Jamie looks down at the floor as he tries to take it in. "That's evil."

"So, you understand why you can't leak any more information back to the Collective? I get why you thought you were doing a good thing, but the situation has changed. You have to help us now. Here, in the Resistance."

When Jamie looks up at me, there's a new determination in his eyes. "I will. I promise."

"Then we have a deal."

"Thanks, Zac. I owe you."

"Don't you forget it."

At that moment, the door swings open and Kieran strolls in, whistling. He pauses when he sees us standing there, my hands on Jamie's shoulders.

"Having fun, boys?" he smirks, as he makes his way to a cubicle. "Don't let me stop you."

"It's ok," I say. "I think we're done here."

And we are.

Jamie and I know where we stand; I've cemented our friendship with my silence.

But at what cost?

TWENTY-SEVEN

The bar is still full of people as I make my way over to the small booth. I stretch out on one of the padded seats, not sitting, but not lying down either. It's too hot to climb inside a sleeping bag. Besides, I'm too anxious to sleep.

I listen to fingers tapping at keyboards and voices murmuring, hoping the familiar noises will calm me.

It's not long before Kieran joins me, sliding in to the seat opposite. "You okay?"

I shake my head. "Not really. I thought when we got here, we'd feel safe. Now I'm wondering if we did the right thing coming back. Layla sounds mad."

He shrugs. "Layla's always mad."

"But what if she hands us over to Cypher?

What happens then?"

"She'd never do it."

"But what if she does? You told me before that Cypher is a psycho. Even you were scared of him."

Kieran doesn't deny it, and that's worrying in itself. "He is pretty hardcore," he mutters.

We sit there in silence, contemplating our fate.

The door slams and Layla storms into the bar area. "Listen up, everyone. We have a potential breach. There are signs of police activity outside. We think they're on to us. Initiate the Blackout protocol immediately."

That gets everyone moving. Hackers dash from one workstation to another, typing in commands, formatting hard drives, deleting evidence, covering their tracks.

"Why are the police here?" I ask, confused. "That makes no sense."

"That's what I want to know," demands Layla.

"Maybe Cypher gave them the location?" suggests Kieran. "His way of punishing this branch of the Resistance for what we did."

Layla gives a small shake of her head. "Cypher would never turn us in to the authorities. We know too much about the Resistance. Besides, he gave us twenty-four hours to turn you in."

"So, what are you saying?" asks Kieran, confused.

"I'm saying that you boys and Trix get back here and within a few hours we have the police breathing down our necks. Hell of a coincidence, wouldn't you say?"

Kieran's still trying to make sense of it. "You think they followed us?"

"Either that or Zac here is not as loyal to the Resistance as he's making out." Layla grabs me by the wrist and pulls me off the seat. "Cypher warned me that the Collective had turned you. I should have listened."

I can't believe what I'm hearing. "You think I did this? You think I told the police where to find us? Why would I?"

"Maybe you're a double agent."

"If that was true, why wouldn't I give them your location while I was still in Arcadia? Think about it! It doesn't make sense. I don't need to be here in person to give away the location of the base."

Layla glares at me, as if she wants to argue, but

she can't fault my logic. "Maybe they're tracking you."

"We were both searched," points out Kieran. "Gavin checked us."

"He might have missed something."

"Or is it possible that this has nothing to do with us?" I pull away from Layla's grasp. "We didn't compromise the location, okay? We can figure out how they found us later. Right now, we need to work out how to escape."

"The boy's right," says Del, heading over, a shotgun in hand. "This ain't the time to point fingers. It's time to stand our ground."

"We can't fight them off with weapons, Del," says Layla.

"Ain't planning to. Just hold them off long enough for you's all ter get away. If I can give 'em enough to think about outside, then maybe some of the gang can slip past to the bikes."

"It could work."

BANG!

An explosion shakes the building, a cloud of smoke billowing towards us from the far end of the room.

"They've blown the bloomin' doors!" yells Del.

"Take cover!"

He grabs me by my shirt and pushes me behind the bar. He crouches down, loading the shotgun. The dust cloud is so thick I can barely see him, let alone what's happening anywhere else in the pub. I hear Kieran coughing nearby.

"Where did Layla go?" I ask him.

"Upstairs," he splutters.

A tinny voice booms out over the chaos: "THIS IS THE POLICE. YOU ARE IN BREACH OF LOCKDOWN REGULATIONS. COME OUT WITH YOUR HANDS UP."

Del stands up, hoisting his shotgun over the bar. "How about you gerrout o' ma pub before I blow you to smithereens!"

He fires the shotgun.

"Are you crazy?" I hiss at him. "You can't shoot the police!"

"It was a warning shot at the ceiling," he hisses back. "But it might make them think twice about coming in. You boys get down to the cellar and try to escape out the back."

Del turns and fires again. At that moment, the power goes out. Fortunately, Kieran and I have lived in the pub for long enough to find our way in the darkness.

"Come on." I tug on Kieran's sweatshirt, pulling him towards the door.

He holds back. "I can't, Zac. I have to find Trix. I can't leave her."

"This is no time to be a hero. She's capable of looking after herself."

Kieran pulls his arm away. "You go ahead. I'll meet you outside."

So, now I'm on my own. I scurry across the floor, trying to stay out of the beam of a flashlight the police are sweeping around the pub. As I crawl over the filthy carpet, I collide heads with someone else.

"Zac? Is that you?" It's Jamie.

"Yeah. Come on. We have to get out." We scramble to the door that leads to the cellar. More shots are fired. One of them is the shotgun. The other is from a different weapon.

"Is that the best yer got?" I hear Del yell. He sounds like he's enjoying himself, but he won't be able to hold them off for long.

I'm gasping for breath by the time we reach the cellar, partly from exertion and partly from adrenaline. We dart down the steps; I almost miss my footing, but Jamie grabs me. Now would be a really bad time to break a leg.

Jamie might be helping me out, but I still turn on him. "Did you give our location to the cops?"

"I gave it to the Collective ages ago. Only a week after you went to Arcadia."

I swear and push him away. I realise I already knew that. "Do you know what you've done?"

"It was before I knew you were the good guys, remember?"

"So, why did they come now?" I say. I'm asking myself as much as Jamie. "If they've had that information for ages, why invade our headquarters tonight?"

Jamie says what I'm thinking. "Because you're here."

He's right. I'm the only one who really knows what's going on in Arcadia. And I'm the one who destroyed the first batch of the vaccine. Maybe they're trying to stop me telling anyone else what I know? Or maybe they just want revenge?

Either way, it's not good.

We race down the narrow corridor. With any luck, the authorities won't know about the beer cellar or the secret hatch. There's still a chance we can get out of this. Or that's what I'm stupid enough to think.

As soon as I push open the hatch, rough hands grab hold of me and lift me into the air. A police officer in a virus protection suit peers out from behind his visor. "Look what I found."

I swing my foot towards his privates, hoping the pain will make him let go, but he's ready for a fight and steps to the side just in time. He twists me round and holds me tight while his colleague gets hold of Jamie.

"Let me go!" I squirm in the man's grasp.

"What have you got there?" Another officer shines a bright light in our faces, making us blink.

"Two kids, by the look of it," says the man holding me. "Shall I put them in the prison van with the others?"

"No, we have special instructions. Anyone under the age of eighteen is to shipped to a different facility up north."

My captor grunts. "Can we at least knock these boys out? They're wriggling like ferrets."

"Afraid not. They don't want any excess chemicals in their system. Take them to the quarantine van and put them in a holding cube."

"We haven't done anything," insists Jamie, but the officer ignores him.

They push us towards a large van parked on the main road.

The back doors are wide open, revealing a clean and clinical interior. On either side are two rows of glass cubes, five deep by two high. They're all empty.

The man who has hold of Jamie swings one box open and pushes him inside. The door slams shut, trapping him in a transparent prison.

"Now it's your turn," says the guy who's holding me.

He forces me forward while his colleague opens up the cube. Once I'm inside, they seal it. There's less space in here than there was in the crates.

There's a few minutes of silence where everyone ignores us.

Then, I watch with horror as Kieran and Trix are dragged in and each given a box of their own. Now, all four of us are prisoners.

We might have blown up the vaccine, but our days fighting for the Resistance are over.

We've been well and truly caught.
And now, we'll pay the price.

EPILOGUE

What was the point?

As I huddle in the cube, I can't help feeling depressed.

When I escaped from Arcadia, I thought I could mobilise the Resistance to rise against the Collective. That somehow Layla and the others would put an end to the fake vaccine, once and for all.

Instead, all I've done is slow things down.

Sure, it will take a few months for the Collective to produce more of the lethal vaccine. We bought the world some time.

But will it matter?

Not really.

There's no point delaying the inevitable.

Now that we've been caught, and our

Resistance cell has been crushed, no one will stop the Collective next time.

My mum will die.

So will my brother.

And who knows what they'll do to me when we get to Arcadia.

My name is Zac, and I did my best. Honestly, I did.

It just wasn't enough.

Now, everyone will suffer.

Including me.

FIND OUT WHAT HAPPENS NEXT:

They have control.

He's their prisoner.

Tortured and trapped, Zac has no hope of escape.

But he can't give up now. The fate of the free world is in his hands. Unless he stops them, the Collective will release a lethal vaccine. Millions will die, including his family.

Everyone thinks he's failed, but he's just getting

started.

This boy has had enough.

Want to know when it's released? Sign up to my readers' club for updates, free books and more!

Check out www.paulorton.net for more details.

A NOTE FROM THE AUTHOR

Thanks for reading *The Fall of Freedom*. I'll soon be releasing the final book in the Lockdown series: *The Age of Arcadia*. If you want to be kept informed when it's released then check out www.paulorton.net.

You may also want to get hold of my other books: the *Ryan Jacobs* series. If you like teenagers with attitude, you'll love Ryan Jacobs! You can even download the prequel to the series completely free on my website.

But first, could you do me a huge favour? I'd love you to review *The Fall of Freedom* on Amazon. Reviews make a huge difference to an independent author like me, and it would be amazing if you could write a sentence or two about what you liked about it. I'd really appreciate it and I promise I read <u>every</u> review.

Until next time,

Paul.

GET YOUR FREE EBOOK

There are traps you can't escape.

When Ryan Jacobs asks to join the Faction he finds himself trapped in a situation which keeps getting worse. He needs to escape fast, or they will own him forever. But how can he fight an invisible enemy?

Find out about Ryan's life before he is taken to the Academy. DARK WEB is exclusively available to those in my readers' club – sign up for free at www.paulorton.net

RYAN JACOBS BOOK 1

Somehow, he lost his freedom.

Now he belongs to the Academy, and the rules have changed. What started out as a game has become a matter of life and death.

If he doesn't think fast, someone will die.

At thirteen you shouldn't have to face these kinds of issues. But at thirteen, you don't get to decide the rules.

THE RULES is the first book in the Ryan Jacobs series and is <u>AVAILABLE NOW ON AMAZON</u>!

RYAN JACOBS BOOK 2

They call it the Fury. And no one is safe.

Life has got very complicated for Ryan. The fact is that he's never been much of a team player. It's not easy when your friends hate you and everyone else is on your case.

And that was before people started going crazy. He has to find some answers, and fast. Before things get out of hand. Before anyone gets killed. Or worse.

WILD FURY is the second book in the Ryan Jacobs series and is <u>AVAILABLE NOW ON AMAZON!</u>

RYAN JACOBS BOOK 3

There's something in the woods.
And it's out of control.

When Ryan realises the danger, he has a difficult decision to make: it's not easy to own up to your mistakes when you're already in so much trouble. But if he doesn't, someone could die.

Will he be able to tame the technology before anyone is killed? Or will he confess and lose his place at the academy? At thirteen, it's a harsh choice. But, this time, he only has himself to blame.

CODE ZERO is the third book in the Ryan Jacobs series and is <u>AVAILABLE NOW ON AMAZON!</u>

RYAN JACOBS BOOK 4

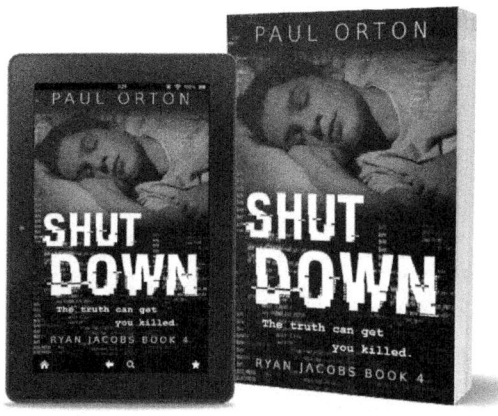

Everyone has secrets.
Even those you least expect.

Ryan is in trouble. He has to stop the shutdown but doesn't know who to trust. The authorities are closing in and he's running out of time. It's not easy being thirteen and having a reputation. Whatever he does, his enemies are one step ahead.

Will he uncover the truth? And will anyone believe him if he does?

SHUT DOWN is the fourth book in the Ryan Jacobs series and is <u>AVAILABLE NOW ON AMAZON!</u>

RYAN JACOBS BOOK 5

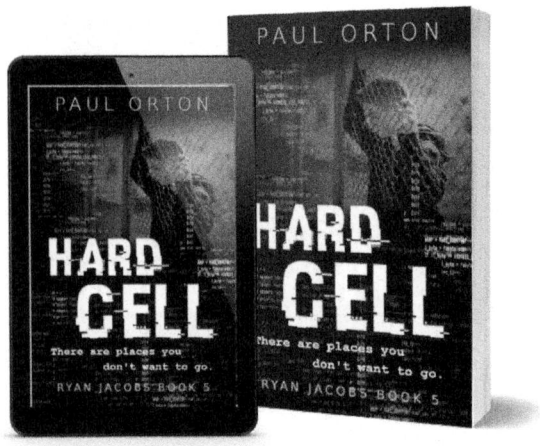

It's the place everyone fears.
Now, he knows why.

Ryan is out of his depth. He's been forced to confess to a crime he didn't commit, and even his friends think he's betrayed them. Worse still, he's been taken to Blackfell, a top-secret prison for teenagers. And the governor is determined to make him suffer.

Will he ever escape? And will he be able to prove his innocence? Or is he destined to spend the rest of his teenage years behind bars?

HARD CELL is the fifth book in the Ryan Jacobs series and is <u>AVAILABLE NOW ON AMAZON!</u>

Printed in Great Britain
by Amazon